She couldn't lo[...]

If Ryder had his wa[...] the practice and mo[...] sheriff's department[...] [...]o know he was concerned fo[...] [...]ouldn't live like that. "I'll be careful," she said. "It's all any of us can do."

He nodded. "That doesn't mean I won't worry."

"And I think your worrying is sweet. It means a lot to me knowing you care. But it unsettles me a little, too. I'm not used to that."

He covered her hands with his own. "I hope you could get used to it."

"Maybe I can. But I need time. And I need space, too. Okay?"

He looked into her eyes. Searching for what? she wondered. He stepped back. "Okay," he said. "I'll walk you to your car, then I have to get back to work. I won't rest easy until we've found this guy."

ICE COLD KILLER

CINDI MYERS

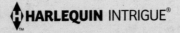

HARLEQUIN INTRIGUE®

Recycling programs
for this product may
not exist in your area.

ISBN-13: 978-1-335-60429-3

Ice Cold Killer

This edition published by arrangement with Harlequin Books S.A.

For questions and comments about the quality of this book, please contact us at CustomerService@Harlequin.com.

Printed in U.S.A.

www.Harlequin.com

Cindi Myers is the author of more than fifty novels. When she's not crafting new romance plots, she enjoys skiing, gardening, cooking, crafting and daydreaming. A lover of small-town life, she lives with her husband and two spoiled dogs in the Colorado mountains.

Books by Cindi Myers

Harlequin Intrigue

Eagle Mountain Murder Mystery: Winter Storm Wedding

Ice Cold Killer

Eagle Mountain Murder Mystery

Saved by the Sheriff
Avalanche of Trouble
Deputy Defender
Danger on Dakota Ridge

The Ranger Brigade: Family Secrets

Murder in Black Canyon
Undercover Husband
Manhunt on Mystic Mesa
Soldier's Promise
Missing in Blue Mesa
Stranded with the Suspect

The Men of Search Team Seven

Colorado Crime Scene
Lawman on the Hunt
Christmas Kidnapping
PhD Protector

Visit the Author Profile page at Harlequin.com.

CAST OF CHARACTERS

Ryder Stewart—This Colorado highway patrolman likes uncomplicated relationships and a simple life—but a serial killer and a certain attractive veterinarian have suddenly complicated everything for him.

Darcy Marsh—The veterinarian has found the peace and security that have long eluded her in the quiet town of Eagle Mountain, but the death of her business partner and threats from an unknown assailant have her questioning everything.

Kelly Farrow—Darcy's best friend and business partner is the killer's first victim.

Ken Rutledge—Kelly's next-door neighbor dated Darcy until she ended the relationship.

Ed Nichols—Eagle Mountain's only veterinarian until Kelly and Darcy arrived. He resents the newcomers, who are cutting into his business.

Alex Woodruff and Tim Dawson—Two college students who came to town to ice climb and got trapped by the weather.

Greg Eicklebaum, Gus Elcott and Pi Calendri—Three high school students who may know more about the killings than they've revealed to the police.

Chapter One

Snow hid a lot of things, Colorado State Patrol Trooper Ryder Stewart mused as he watched the wrecker back up to the white, box-shaped clump near the top of Dixon Pass. Christy O'Brien, a sturdy blonde with chin-length hair beneath a bright red knit beanie, stopped the wrecker a few inches from the snow clump, climbed out and brushed at the flakes with a gloved hand, revealing the bumper of a brown delivery truck. She knelt and hooked chains underneath the truck, then gave Ryder a thumbs-up. "Ready to go."

Ryder glanced behind him at the barrier he'd set up over the highway, and the Road Closed sign just beyond it. Ahead of Ryder, a cascade of snow flowed over the pavement, part of the avalanche that had trapped the truck. "You're clear," he said.

Slowly, Christy eased the wrecker forward. With a sound like two pieces of foam rubbing together, the delivery truck emerged from its icy cocoon. When the truck was fully on the pavement, the wrecker stopped. The door to the delivery truck slid open, clumps of snow hitting the pavement with a muffled *floof.* "Took you long enough!" Alton Reed grinned as he said the words and brushed snow from the shoulders of his brown jacket.

"How many times is this, Alton?" Ryder asked, looking the driver up and down.

"First one this year—fourth overall." Alton surveyed the truck. "Got buried pretty deep this time. I'm thinking it's going to be a bad year for avalanches."

"The weather guessers say it's going to be a bad snow year." Ryder studied the pewter sky, heavy clouds like dirty cotton sitting low on the horizon. "This is the second time this week we've had to close the highway. Might not open again for a few days if the weather keeps up."

"You people ought to be used to it," Alton said. "It happens often enough. Though I can't say I'd care for being cut off from the rest of the world that way."

"Only four days last winter," Ryder said.

"And what—three weeks the year before that?"

"Three years ago, but yeah." Ryder shrugged. "The price we pay for living in paradise." That was how most people who lived there thought of Eagle Mountain, anyway—a small town in a gorgeous setting that outsiders flocked to every summer and fall. The fact that there was only one way in and out of the town, and that way was sometimes blocked by avalanches in the winter, only added to the appeal for some.

"Guess I'll have to find a place in town to stay

until the weather clears," Alton said, eyeing the cascade of snow that spilled across the highway in front of them.

"You ever think of asking for a different route?" Ryder asked. "One that isn't so avalanche prone?"

"Nah." Alton climbed back into his van. "After the first scare, it's kind of an adrenaline rush, once you realize you're going to be okay. And this route includes hazard pay—a nice bonus."

Ryder waved goodbye as Alton turned his truck and steered around the barriers, headed toward town. He and the other commuting workers, delivery drivers and tourists trapped by the storm would find refuge at the local motel and B&Bs. Ryder shifted his attention to Christy, who was fiddling with the chains on her wrecker. "Thanks, Christy," he said. "Maybe I won't have to call you out anymore today."

"Don't you want me to pull out the other vehicle?" she asked.

The words gave him a jolt. "Other vehicle?" He turned to stare at the snowbank, and was stunned to see a glint of red, like the shine of a taillight. The vehicle it belonged to must have been right up against the rock face. Alton hadn't mentioned it, so he must not have known it was there, either. "Yeah, you'd better pull it out, too," he said. "Do you need any help?"

"No, I've got it."

He shoved his hands in the pockets of his fleece-lined, leather patrolman's jacket and blew out a cloud of breath as he waited for Christy to secure the vehicle. When she'd brushed away some of the snow, he could make out a small sedan with Colorado plates.

Wedged farther back under the packed snow, the car took longer to extricate, but it was lighter than the delivery van, and Christy's wrecker had tire chains and a powerful engine. She dragged the vehicle, the top dented in from the weight of the snow, onto the pavement.

Snow fell away from the car, revealing a slumped form inside. Ryder raced to the vehicle and tried the door. It opened when he pulled hard, and he leaned in to take a look, then groped for the radio on his shoulder. "I need an ambulance up at the top of Dixon Pass," he said. "And call the medical examiner."

Even before he reached out to feel for the woman's pulse, he knew she wouldn't be needing that ambulance. The young, brown-haired woman was as cold as the snow that surrounded them, her hands and feet bound with silver duct tape, her throat slit all the way across.

He leaned back out of the car and tilted his head up into the cold, welcoming the feel of icy flakes on his cheeks. Yeah, the snow hid a lot of things, not all of them good.

DARCY MARSH RAN her fingers through the silky fur of the squirming Labrador puppy, and grinned as a soft pink tongue swiped at her cheek. For all the frustrations that were part of being a veterinarian, visits like this were one of the perks. "I'd say Admiral is a fine, healthy pup," she told the beaming couple in front of her. High school teacher Maya Renfro and Sheriff's Deputy Gage Walker returned the smile. "We'll keep an eye on that little umbilical hernia, but I don't expect it will cause any problems."

"Can Casey hold him now?" Maya asked, smiling at her young niece, Casey, who was deaf. The little girl's busily signing fingers conveyed her eagerness to cuddle her puppy.

"Yes, I think he's ready to come down." Darcy handed over the pup, and Casey cradled him carefully.

"You'll need to bring him back in a month for his second set of puppy vaccinations," Darcy said as she washed her hands at the exam room sink. "If you have any concerns before then, don't hesitate to give us a call."

"Thanks, Doc," Gage said. The family followed Darcy to the front of the office. "Are you all by yourself today?"

"It's Dr. Farrow's day off," Darcy said. "And I let Stacy go early, since you're my last client for today."

"Not quite the last," Maya said. She nodded toward the open waiting room door. An auburn-haired man in the blue shirt and tan slacks of a Colorado State Patrolman stood at their approach.

"Ryder, what are you doing here?" Gage asked, stepping forward to shake hands with the trooper.

"I just needed to talk to the vet for a minute," the officer, Ryder, said. He looked past Gage. "Hello, Maya, Casey. That's a good-looking pup you have there."

"His name is Admiral," Maya said as Casey walked forward with the now squirming dog.

Ryder knelt and patted the puppy. "I'll bet you two have a lot of fun together," he said, speaking slowly so that Casey could read his lips.

Darcy moved to the office computer and printed out an invoice for Maya, who paid while Gage and Ryder made small talk about dogs, the weather and the upcoming wedding of Gage's brother, Sheriff Travis Walker. "We're thinking of throwing some kind of bachelor party thing in a couple of weeks," Gage said. "I'll let you know when I have all the details. We may have to stay in town, if the weather keeps up like this."

"That should be an exciting party—not," Maya said as she returned her wallet to her purse. "All the local law enforcement gathered at Moe's pub, with the entire town keeping tabs on your behavior."

"This is my brother we're talking about," Gage said. "Travis isn't exactly known for cutting loose."

Laughing, they said goodbye to Ryder and left.

"What can I do for you?" Darcy leaned back against her front counter and studied the trooper. He was young, fit and good-looking, with closely cropped dark auburn hair and intense blue eyes. She had only been in Eagle Mountain four months, but how had she missed running into him? She certainly wouldn't have forgotten a guy this good-looking.

"Are you Dr. Darcy Marsh?" he asked.

"Yes."

"Is Kelly Farrow your business partner?"

"Yes." The room suddenly felt at least ten degrees colder. Darcy gripped the edges of the front counter. "Is something wrong?" she asked. "Has Kelly been in an accident?" Her partner had a bit of a reckless streak. She always drove too fast, and with this weather…

"I'm sorry to have to tell you that Ms. Farrow—Dr. Farrow—is dead," Ryder said.

Darcy stared at him, the words refusing to sink in. Kelly…dead?

"Why don't you sit down?" Ryder took her by the arm and gently led her to a chair in the waiting room, then walked over and flipped the sign on the door to Closed. He filled a paper cup with water from the cooler by the door and brought it to her. At any other time, she might have objected to him taking charge that way, but she didn't see the point at the moment.

She sipped water and tried to pull herself together. "Kelly's really dead?" she asked.

"I'm afraid so." He pulled a second chair over and sat facing her. "I need to ask you some questions about her."

"What happened?" Darcy asked. "Was she in an accident? I always warned her about driving so fast. She—"

"It wasn't an accident," he said.

She made herself look at him then, into eyes that were both sympathetic and determined. Not unkind eyes, but his expression held a hint of steel. Trooper Stewart wasn't a man to be messed with. She swallowed hard, and somehow found her voice. "If it wasn't an accident, how did she die?" Did Kelly have some kind of undiagnosed heart condition or something?

"She was murdered."

Darcy gasped, and her vision went a little fuzzy around the edges. This must be a nightmare—one of those super-vivid dreams that felt like real life, but wasn't. This couldn't possibly be real.

Then she was aware of cold water soaking into her slacks, and Ryder gently taking the paper cup from her hand. "I need to ask you some questions that may help me find her murderer," he said.

"How?" she asked. "I mean, how was she… killed?" The word was hard to say.

"We don't have all the details yet," he said. "She was found in her car, buried in an avalanche on top of Dixon Pass. Do you know why she might have been up there?"

Why wasn't her brain working better? Nothing he said made sense to her. She brushed at the damp spot on her pants and tried to put her thoughts into some coherent order. "She told me she was going shopping and to lunch in Junction," she said. Leaving Eagle Mountain meant driving over Dixon Pass. There was no other way in or out.

"When was the last time you spoke to her?" Ryder asked.

"Yesterday afternoon, when we both left work. Today was her day off."

"Was that unusual, for her to take off during the week?"

"No. We each take one day off during the week so we can both work Saturdays. My day off is Wednesday. Hers is Tuesday."

"How long have you known her?"

Darcy frowned, trying to concentrate. "Five years? We met in college, then were roommates in vet school. We really hit it off. When she was looking for a partner to start a vet business here in Eagle Mountain, I jumped at the chance."

"Are you still roommates?" he asked.

"No. She lives in a duplex in town and I have a place just outside town—on the Lusk Ranch, out on County Road Three."

"Do you know of anyone who would want to hurt her?" he asked. "Does she have a history of a stalker, or someone from her past she's had a rocky relationship with?"

"No! Kelly got along with everyone." Darcy swallowed past the lump in her throat and pinched her hand, hard, trying to snap out of the fog his news had put her in. She couldn't break down now. Not yet. "If you had ever met her, you'd understand. She was this outgoing, sunny, super-friendly person. I was the more serious, quiet one. She used to say we were good business partners because we each brought different strengths to the practice." She buried her face in her hands. "What am I going to do without her?"

"Can you think of anyone at all she might have argued with recently—an unhappy client, perhaps?"

Darcy shook her head. "No. We've only been open a few months—less than four. So far all our interactions with clients have been good ones. I know, realistically, that won't last. You can't please everyone. But it's been a good experience so far. Well, except for Dr. Nichols." She made a face.

"Ed Nichols, the other vet in town?"

"Yes." She sighed. "He wasn't happy about our coming here. He said there wasn't enough business in a town this small for one vet, much less three. He accused us of undercutting his prices, and then I heard from some patients that he's been bad-mouthing us around town. But he never threatened us or anything like that. I mean, I can't believe he would want to kill one of us." She wrapped her arms around herself, suddenly cold.

"Where were you this morning, from nine to one?" Ryder asked.

"Is that when she died? I was here, seeing patients. We open at eight o'clock."

"Did you go out for lunch?"

"No. We had an emergency call—a dog that had tangled with a porcupine. I had to sedate the poor guy to get the quills out. I ended up eating a granola bar at my desk about one o'clock."

"So you usually spend all day at the office here?"

She shook her head. "Not always. One of us is usually here, but we also treat large animals—horses and cows, mostly, but we see the occasional llama or donkey. Sometimes it's easier to go out to the animal than to have them brought here. That was something else Dr. Nichols didn't like—that we would do house calls like that. He said it set a bad precedent."

"Was Kelly dating anyone?" Ryder asked.

"She dated a lot of people, but no one seriously. She was pretty and outgoing and popular."

"Did she ever mention a man she didn't get along with? A relationship that didn't end well—either here or where you were before?"

"We were in Fort Collins. And no. Kelly got along with everyone." She made dating look easy, and had sometimes teased Darcy—though gently—about her reluctance to get involved.

"What about you? Are you seeing anyone?"

"No." What did that have to do with Kelly? But before she could ask, Ryder stood. He towered over her—maybe six feet four inches tall, with broad shoulders and muscular thighs. She shrank back from his presence, an involuntary action she hated, but couldn't seem to control.

"Can I call someone for you?" he asked. "A friend or relative?"

"No." She grabbed a tissue and pressed it to her eyes. "I need to call Kelly's parents. They'll be devastated."

"Give me their contact information and I'll do that," he said. "It's part of my job. You can call and talk to them later."

"All right." She went to the office, grateful for something to do, and pulled up Kelly's information on the computer. "I'll go over to her house and get her cats," she said. "Is it okay if I do that? I have a key." Kelly had a key to Darcy's place, too. The two looked after each other's pets and were always in and out of each other's homes.

"Yes. I already stopped by her place with an evidence team from the sheriff's department. That's how we found your contact information."

She handed him a piece of paper on which she'd written the names and numbers for Kelly's parents. He took it and gave her a business card. "I wrote my cell number on there," he said. "Call me if you think of anything that might help us. Even something small could be the key to finding out what happened to her."

She stared at the card, her vision blurring, then tucked it in the front pocket of her slacks. "Thank you."

"Are you sure you're going to be okay?" he asked.

No. How could she be okay again, with her best friend dead? And not just dead—murdered. She shook her head but said, "I'll be all right. I'm used to looking after myself."

The intensity in his gaze unnerved her. He seemed genuinely concerned, but she wasn't always good at reading people. "I'll be fine," she said. "And I'll call you if I think of anything."

He left and she went through the motions of closing up. The two cats and a dog in hospital cages were doing well. The dog—the porcupine victim—would be able to go home in the morning, and one of the cats, as well. The other cat, who had had surgery to remove a tumor, was also looking better and should be home by the weekend. She shut down the computer and set the alarm, then locked up behind her.

Outside it was growing dark, snow swirling over the asphalt of the parking lot, the pine trees across the street dusted with snow. The scene might have been one from a Christmas card, but Darcy felt none of the peace she would have before Ryder's visit. Who would want to hurt Kelly? Eagle Mountain had seemed such an idyllic town—a place where a single woman could walk down the street after dark and never feel threatened, where most people didn't bother to lock their doors, where children walked to school without fear. After only four months she knew more people here than she had in six years in Fort Collins. Kelly had made friends with almost everyone.

Was her killer one of those friends? Or a random stranger she had been unfortunate enough to cross paths with? That sort of thing was supposed to happen in cities, not way out here in the middle of nowhere. Maybe Eagle Mountain was just another ugly place in a pretty package, and the peace she had thought she had found was just a lie.

Chapter Two

A half mile from the veterinary clinic, Ryder almost turned around and went back. Leaving Darcy Marsh alone hadn't felt right, despite all her insisting that he go. But what was he going to do for her in her grief? He'd be better off using his time to interview Ed Nichols. Maybe he would call Darcy later and check that she was okay. She was so quiet. So self-contained. He was like that himself, but there was something else going on with her. She hadn't been afraid of him, but he had sensed her discomfort with him. Something more than her grief was bothering her. Was it because he was law enforcement? Because he was a man? Something else?

He didn't like unanswered questions. It was one of the things that made him a good investigator. He liked figuring people out—why they acted the way they did. If he hadn't been a law enforcement officer, he might have gone into psychology, except that sitting in an office all day would have driven him batty. He needed to be active and *doing*.

Ed Nichols lived in a small, ranch-style home with

dark green cedar siding and brick-red trim. Giant blue spruce trees at the corners dwarfed the dwelling, and must have cast it in perpetual shadow. In the winter twilight, lights glowed from every window as if determined to dispel the gloom. Ryder parked his Chevy Tahoe at the curb and strode up the walk. Somewhere inside the house, a dog barked. Before he could ring the bell, the door opened and a man in his midfifties, thick blond hair fading to white, answered the door. "Is something wrong?" he asked.

"Dr. Nichols?" Ryder asked.

"Yes?" The man frowned.

"I need to speak with you a moment."

Toenails clicking on the hardwood floors announced the arrival of not one dog, but two—a small white poodle and a large, curly-haired mutt. The mutt stared at Ryder, then let out a loud *woof.*

"Hush, Murphy," Dr. Nichols said. He caught the dog by the collar and held him back, the poodle cowering behind, and pushed open the storm door. "You'd better come in."

A woman emerged from the back of the house— a trim brunette in black yoga pants and a purple sweater. She paled when she saw Ryder. "Is something wrong? Our son?"

"I'm not here about your son," Ryder said quickly. He turned to Nichols. "I wanted to ask you some questions about Kelly Farrow."

"Kelly?" Surprise, then suspicion, clouded Nichols's expression. He lowered himself into the recliner and began stroking the big dog's head while the little one settled in his lap. "What about her?"

"You might as well sit down," Mrs. Nichols said. She perched on the edge of an adjacent love seat while Ryder took a seat on the sofa. "When was the last time you saw Kelly Farrow?" he asked.

Nichols frowned. "I don't know. Maybe—last week? I think I passed her on the street. Why? What is this about? Is she saying I've done something?"

"What would she say you've done?"

"Nothing! I don't have anything to do with those two."

"Those two?"

"Kelly and that other girl, Darcy."

"I understand you weren't too happy about them opening a new practice in Eagle Mountain."

"Who told you that?"

"Is it true?"

Nichols focused on the big dog, running his palm from the top of its head to the tip of its tail, over and over. "A town this small only needs one vet. But they're free to do as they please."

"Has your own business suffered since they opened their practice?" Ryder asked.

"What does that have to do with anything?" Mrs. Nichols spoke, leaning toward Ryder. "Are you accusing my husband of something?"

"You can't come into my home and start asking all these questions without telling us why," Nichols said.

"Kelly Farrow is dead. I'm trying to find out who killed her."

Nichols stared, his mouth slightly open. "Dead?"

"Ed certainly didn't kill her," Mrs. Nichols protested. "Just because he might have criticized the woman doesn't mean he's a murderer."

"Sharon, you're not helping," Nichols said.

"Where were you between nine and one today?" Ryder asked.

"I was at my office." He nodded to his wife. "Sharon can confirm that. She's my office manager."

"He saw patients all morning and attended the Rotary Club meeting at lunch," Sharon said.

"Listen, Kelly wasn't my favorite person in the world, but I wouldn't do something like that," Nichols said. "I couldn't."

Ryder wanted to believe the man, who seemed genuinely shaken, but it was too early in the case to make judgments of guilt or innocence. His job now was to gather as many facts as possible. He stood. "I may need to see your appointment book and talk to some of your clients to verify your whereabouts," he said.

"This is appalling." Sharon also rose, her cheeks flushed, hands clenched into fists. "How dare you accuse my husband this way."

"I'm not accusing him of anything," Ryder said. "It's standard procedure to check everyone's alibis." He nodded to Nichols. "Someone from my office will be in touch."

Ryder left the Nicholses' and headed back toward Main. He passed a familiar red-and-white wrecker, and Christy O'Brien tooted her horn and waved.

Weather like this always meant plenty of work for Christy and her dad, pulling people out of ditches and jump-starting cars whose batteries had died in the cold.

Ryder pulled into the grocery store lot and parked. He could see a few people moving around inside the lit store—employees who had to be there, he guessed. People who didn't have to be out in this weather stayed home. The automatic doors at the store entrance opened and a trio of teenage boys emerged, bare-headed and laughing, their letter jackets identifying them as students at the local high school. Apparently, youth was immune to the weather. They sauntered across the lot to a dark gray SUV and piled in.

Ryder contacted his office in Grand Junction to update them on his progress with the case. Since state patrol personnel couldn't reach him because of the closed road, he had called on the sheriff's department to process the crime scene. After the medical examiner had arrived at the scene and the ambulance had transported the body to the funeral home that would serve as a temporary morgue, he had had Kelly's car towed to the sheriff's department impound lot. But none of the forensic evidence—blood and hair samples, fingerprints and DNA—could be processed until the roads opened again. Eagle Mountain didn't have the facilities to handle such evidence.

"The highway department is saying the road won't open until day after tomorrow at the earliest," the duty officer told Ryder. "It could be longer, depending on the weather."

"Meanwhile, the trail gets colder," Ryder said. "And if the killer is on the other side of the pass, he has plenty of time to get away while I sit here waiting for the weather to clear."

"Do what you can. We'll run a background check on this Ed Nichols and let you know what we find. We're also doing a search for similar crimes."

"I'm going to talk to the sheriff, see if he has any suspects I haven't uncovered."

He ended the call and sat, staring out across the snowy lot and contemplating his next move. He could call it a night and go home, but he doubted he would get any rest. In a murder investigation it was important to move quickly, while the evidence was still fresh. But the weather had him stymied. Still, there must be more he could do.

A late-model Toyota 4Runner cruised slowly through the parking lot, a young man behind the wheel. He passed Ryder's Tahoe, his face a blur behind snow-flecked glass, then turned back out of the lot. Was he a tourist, lost and using the lot to turn around? Or a bored local, out cruising the town? Ryder hadn't recognized the vehicle, and after two years in Eagle Mountain, he knew most people. But new folks moved in all the time, many of them second homeowners who weren't around enough to get to know. And even this time of year there were tourists, drawn to backcountry skiing and ice climbing.

Any one of them might be a murderer. Was Kelly

Farrow the killer's only victim, or merely the first? The thought would keep Ryder awake until he had answers.

DARCY PARKED IN front of Kelly's half of the duplex off Fifth Street. Kelly had liked the place because it was within walking distance of the clinic, with easy access to the hiking trails along the river. Darcy let herself in with her key and when she flicked on the light, an orange tabby stared at her from the hall table, tail flicking. *Meow!*

"Hello, Pumpkin." Darcy scratched behind the cat's ears, and Pumpkin pressed his head into her palm.

Mroww! This more insistent cry came from a sleek, cream-colored feline, seal-point ears attesting to a Siamese heritage.

"Hello, Spice." Darcy knelt, one hand extended. Spice deigned to let her pet her.

Darcy stood and looked around at the evidence that someone else—Ryder, she guessed—had been here. Mail was spread out in a messy array on the hall table, and powdery residue—fingerprint powder?—covered the door frame and other surfaces. Darcy moved farther into the house, noting the afghan crumpled at the bottom of the sofa, a paperback romance novel splayed, spine up, on the table beside it. A rectangle outlined by dust on the desk in the corner of the room indicated where Kelly's laptop had sat. Ryder had probably taken it. From television crime dramas she had watched, she guessed he would look at her emails and other correspondence, searching for threats or any indication that someone had wanted to harm Kelly.

But Kelly would have said something to Darcy if anyone had threatened her. Unlike Darcy, Kelly never held back her feelings. Darcy blinked back stinging tears and hurried to the kitchen, to the cat carriers stacked in the corner. Both cats watched from the doorway, tails twitching, suspicious.

She set the open carriers in the middle of the kitchen floor, then filled two dishes with the gourmet salmon Pumpkin and Spice favored, and slid the dishes into the carrier. Pumpkin took the bait immediately, scarcely looking up from devouring the food when Darcy fastened the door of the carrier. Spice was more wary, tail twitching furiously as she prowled around the open carrier. But hunger won over caution and soon she, too, darted inside, and Darcy fastened the door.

She was loading the second crate into the back of her Subaru when the door to the other half of the duplex opened. A man's figure filled the doorway. "Darcy, is that you?"

"Hello, Ken." She tried to relax some of the stiffness from her face as she turned to greet Kelly's neighbor. Ken Rutledge was a trim, athletic man who taught math and coached boys' track and Junior Varsity basketball at Eagle Mountain High School.

He came toward her and she forced herself not to pull away when he took her arm. "What's going on?" he asked. "When I got home from practice two cop cars were pulling away from Kelly's half of the house." He looked past her to the back of her Forester. "And you're taking Kelly's cats? Has something happened to her?"

"Kelly's dead. Someone killed her." Her voice broke, and she let him pull her into his arms.

"Kelly's dead?" he asked, smoothing his hand down her back as she sobbed. "How? Who?"

She hated that she had to fight so hard to pull herself together. She tried to shove out of his arms, but he held her tight. She reminded herself that this was just Ken—Kelly's neighbor, and a man Darcy herself had dated a few times. He thought he was being helpful, holding her this way. She forced herself to relax and wait for her tears to subside. When his hold on her loosened, she eased back. "I don't know any details," she said. "A state patrolman told me they found her up on Dixon Pass—murdered."

"That's horrible." Ken's eyes were bright with the shock of the news—and fascination. "Who would want to hurt Kelly?"

"The cops didn't stop to talk to you?" she asked.

"When I saw the sheriff's department vehicles I didn't pull in," he said. "I drove past and waited until they were gone before I came back."

"Why would you do that?" She stared at him.

He shrugged. "I have a couple of traffic tickets I haven't paid. I didn't want any hassle if they looked me up and saw them."

She took a step back. "Ken, they're going to want to talk to you," she said. "You may know something.

You might have seen someone hanging around here, watching Kelly."

"I haven't seen anything like that." He shoved his hands in his pockets. "And I'll talk to them. I just didn't feel like dealing with them tonight. I mean, I didn't know Kelly was dead."

She closed the hatch of the car. "I have to go," she said.

He put a hand on her shoulder. "You shouldn't be alone at a time like this," he said. "You're welcome to stay with me."

"No. Thank you." She took out her keys and clutched them, automatically lacing them through her fingers to use as a weapon, the way the self-defense instructor in Fort Collins had shown her.

His expression clouded. "If it was someone else, you'd accept help, wouldn't you?" he said. "Because it's me, you're refusing. Just because we have a romantic history, doesn't mean we can't be friends."

She closed her eyes, then opened them to find him glaring at her. Were they ever going to stop having this conversation? They had only gone out together three times. To her, that didn't constitute a *romantic history*, though he insisted on seeing things differently. "Ken, I don't want to talk about this now," she said. "I'm tired and I'm upset and I just want to go home."

"I'm here for you, Darcy," he said.

"I know." She got into the driver's seat, forcing herself not to hurry, and drove away. When she glanced in the rearview mirror, Ken was still standing in the drive, frowning after her, hands clenched into fists at his sides.

Dating him had been a bad idea—Darcy had known it from the first date—but Kelly had pressured her to give him a chance. "He's a nice man," she had said. "And the two of you have a lot in common."

They did have a lot in common—a shared love of books and animals and hiking. But Ken pushed too hard. He wanted too much. After only two dates, he had asked her to move in with him. He had talked about them taking a vacation together next summer, and had wanted her to come home to Wisconsin to meet his parents for Christmas. She had broken off with him then, telling him she wasn't ready to get serious with anyone. He had pretended not to understand, telling her coming home to meet his family was just friendly, not serious. But she couldn't see things that way.

He had been upset at first—angry even. He called her some horrible names and told her she would regret losing a guy like him. But after he had returned from visiting his folks last week, he had been more cordial. They had exchanged greetings when she stopped by to see Kelly, and the three of them spent a couple of hours one afternoon shoveling the driveway together. Darcy had been willing to be friends with him, as long as he didn't want more.

She turned onto the gravel county road that led to the horse ranch that belonged to one of their first clients. Robbie Lusk had built the tiny house on wheels parked by the creek as an experiment, he said, and was happy to rent it out to Darcy. His hope was to add more tiny homes and form a little community, and he had a second home under construction.

Darcy slowed to pull into her drive, her cozy home visible beneath the golden glow of the security light one hundred yards ahead. But she was startled to see a dark SUV moving down the drive toward her. Heart in her throat, she braked hard, eliciting complaints from the cats in their carriers behind her. The SUV barreled out past her, a rooster tail of wet snow in its wake. It turned sharply, scarcely inches from her front bumper, and she tried to see the driver, but could make out nothing in the darkness and swirling snow.

She stared at the taillights of the SUV in her rear-view mirror as it raced back toward town. Then, hands shaking, she pulled out her phone and found the card Ryder had given her. She punched in his number and waited for it to ring. "Ryder Stewart," he answered.

"This is Darcy Marsh. Can you come out to my house? A strange car was here and just left. I didn't recognize it and I… I'm afraid." Her knuckles ached from gripping the phone so hard, and her throat hurt from admitting her fear.

"Stay in your car. I'll be right there," Ryder said, his voice strong and commanding, and very reassuring.

Chapter Three

Ryder met no other cars on the trip to Darcy's house. Following the directions she had given him, he turned into a gravel drive and spotted her Subaru Forester parked in front of a redwood-sided dwelling about the size of a train caboose. She got out of the car when he parked his Tahoe beside her, a slight figure in black boots and a knee-length, black puffy coat, her dark hair uncovered. "I haven't looked around to see if anything was messed with," she said. "I thought I should wait for you."

"Good idea." He took his flashlight from his belt and played it over the ground around the house. It didn't look disturbed, but it was snowing hard enough the flakes might have covered any tracks. "Let me know if you spot anything out of place," he said.

She nodded and, keys in hand, moved to the front door. "I know most people around here don't lock their doors," she said. "But I'm enough of a city girl, I guess, that it's a habit I can't break." She turned the key in the lock and pushed open the door, reaching in to flick on the lights, inside and out.

Ryder followed her inside, in time to see two cats descending the circular stairs from the loft, the smaller, black one bounding down, the larger silver tabby moving at a more leisurely pace. "Hello, guys." Darcy shrugged off her shoulder bag and bent to greet the cats. "The black one is Marianne. Her older sister is Elinor." She glanced up at him through surprisingly long lashes. "The Dashwood sisters. From *Sense and Sensibility.*"

He nodded. "I take it you're a fan of Jane Austen?"

"Yes. Have you read the book?"

"No." He couldn't help feeling he had failed some kind of test as she moved away from him, though she couldn't go far. He could see the entire dwelling, except for the loft and the part of the bathroom not visible through the open door at the end, from this spot by the door—a small sitting area, galley kitchen and table for two. The space was organized, compact and a little claustrophobic. It was a dwelling designed for one person—and two cats.

Make that four cats. "I stopped by Kelly's place and picked up her two cats," she said. "Will you help me bring them in?"

He followed her back to her car and accepted one of the cat carriers. The cat inside, a large gold tabby, eyed him balefully and began to yowl. "Oh, Pumpkin, don't be such a crybaby," Darcy chided as she led the way back up the walk. Inside they set the carriers side by side on the sofa that butted up against the table on one side of the little house. "I'll open the carrier doors and they'll come out when they're ready," she said. "They've stayed here before."

"I'll go outside and take a look around," he said, leaving her to deal with the cats.

A closer inspection showed tire tracks in the soft snow to one side of the gravel drive, and fast-filling-in shoe prints leading around one end of the house to a large back window. He shone the light around the frame, over fresh tool marks, as if someone had tried to jimmy it open. Holding the light in one hand, he took several photos with his phone, then went back inside.

"I put on water for tea," Darcy said, indicating the teakettle on the three-burner stove. "I always feel better with a cup of tea." She rubbed her hands up and down her shoulders. She was still wearing her black puffy coat.

Ryder took out his notebook. "What can you remember about the vehicle you saw?" he asked.

"It was a dark color—dark gray or black, and an SUV, or maybe a small truck with a camper cover? A Toyota, I think." She shook her head. "I'm not a person who pays much attention to cars. It was probably someone who was lost, turning around. I shouldn't have called you."

Ryder thought of the 4Runner that had cruised past him in the grocery store parking lot. "There are fresh footprints leading around the side of the house, and marks on your back window, where someone might have tried to get in."

All color left her face, and she pressed her lips together until they, too, were bleached white. "Show me," she said.

She followed him back out into the snow. He took her arm to steer her around the fading shoe prints, and shone the light on the gouges in the wooden window frame. "I'm sure those weren't here before," she said. "The place was brand-new when I moved in four months ago."

"I'll turn in a report to the sheriff's office," he said. "Have you seen the vehicle you described before?"

"No. But like I said, I don't pay attention to cars. Maybe I should."

"Have you seen any strangers out here? Noticed anyone following you? Has Kelly mentioned anything about anyone following her?"

"No." She turned and walked back into the house. When he stepped in after her, the teakettle was screaming. She moved quickly to shut off the burner and filled two mugs with steaming water. Fear seemed to rise off her like the vapor off the water, though she was trying hard to control it.

"I know this is unsettling," he said. "But the fact that the person didn't stay when you arrived here by yourself tells me he was more likely a burglar who didn't want to be caught, than someone who wanted to attack you."

"I was supposed to be safe here," she said.

"Safe from what?"

She carried both mugs to the table and sat. He

took the seat across from her. "Safe from what?" he asked again. "I'm not asking merely to be nosy. If you have someone you're hiding from—someone who might want to hurt you—it's possible this person confused you and Kelly. It wouldn't be the first time something like that happened."

"No, it's not like that." She tucked her shoulder-length brown hair behind her ear, then brought the mug to her lips, holding it in both hands. When she set it down again, her eyes met his, a new determination in their brown depths. "I was raped in college—in Fort Collins. I moved in with Kelly after that and she really helped me move past that. My mother and I aren't close and my father has been out of the picture for years."

He thought of what she had said before—that she was used to looking after herself. "Women who have been through something like that often have a heightened awareness of danger," he said. "It's good to pay attention to that. Have you seen anyone suspicious, here or at Kelly's or at your office? Have you felt threatened or uneasy?"

"No." She shook her head. "That's why I thought Eagle Mountain was different. I always felt safe here. Until now."

He sipped the tea—something with cinnamon and apples. Not bad. It would be even better with a shot of whiskey, but since he was technically still on duty, he wouldn't bring it up. He wondered if she even had hard liquor in the house. "I stopped by and talked to Ed Nichols and his wife after I left the clinic," he said.

Fine lines between her eyes deepened. "You don't really think he killed Kelly, do you?"

"I haven't made up my mind about anything at this point. He said he was at the clinic all morning, and then at the Rotary Club luncheon."

"How did she die?" Darcy asked. "You told me you found her up on Dixon Pass, but how?"

"Do you really want to know?"

"I have a very good imagination. If you don't tell me, I'll fill in too many horrid details of my own." She took another sip of tea. "Besides, the papers will be full of the story soon."

"She was in her car, over to the side, up against the rock face at the top of the pass. Her hands and feet were bound with duct tape and her throat had been cut."

Darcy let out a ragged breath. "Had she been raped?"

"I don't know. But her clothes weren't torn or disarrayed. We'll know more tomorrow."

"So someone just killed her and left her up there? Why there?"

"I don't know. Maybe he—or she—hoped what did happen would happen—an avalanche buried the car. We might not have found it for weeks if a delivery truck wasn't buried in the same place. When we pulled out the delivery driver, we found Kelly's car, too."

"Did you talk to her parents?"

"Yes. They wanted to fly down right away. I told them they should wait until the road opens."

"When will that be?"

"We don't know. A storm system has settled in. They're predicting up to four feet of new snow. Until it stops, no one is getting in or out of Eagle Mountain."

"The sheriff and Lacy Milligan are supposed to get married in a few weeks," she said.

"The road should be open by then," he said. He hoped so. He wasn't going to get far with this case without the information he could get outside town.

"When I moved here and people told me about the road being closed sometimes in winter, I thought it sounded exciting," she said. "Kind of romantic, even—everyone relying on each other in true pioneer spirit. Then I think about our weekly order of supplies not getting through, and people who don't live here being stuck in motels or doubling up with family—then it doesn't sound like much fun." She looked up at him. "What about you? Do you live here?"

"I do. I'm in a converted carriage house over on Elm."

"No pets? Or are you a client of Dr. Nichols's?"

Her teasing tone lifted his spirits. "No pets," he said. "I like dogs, but my hours would mean leaving it alone too long."

"Cats do better on their own." She turned to watch Pumpkin facing off with Marianne. The two cats sniffed each other from nose to tail then, satisfied, moved toward the stairs and up into the loft.

"I should let you go," she said. "Thank you for stopping by."

"Is there someone you could stay with tonight?" he asked. "Or you could get a motel room, somewhere not so isolated."

"No, I'll be fine." She looked around. "I don't want to leave the cats. I have a gun and I know how to use it. Kelly and I took a class together. It helped me feel stronger."

He was tempted to say he would stay here tonight, but he suspected she wouldn't welcome the offer. He'd have to sleep sitting up on her little sofa, or freeze in his Tahoe. "Keep your phone with you and call 911 if you feel at all uneasy," he said.

"I will. I guess I should have called them in the first place."

"I wasn't saying I minded coming out here. I didn't. I don't. If you feel better calling me, don't hesitate."

She nodded. "I guess I called you because I knew you. I'm not always comfortable with strangers."

"I'm glad you trusted me enough to call me. And I meant it—don't think twice about calling me again."

"All right. And I'll be fine." Her smile was forced, but he admired the effort.

He glanced in the rearview mirror as he drove away, at the little house in the snowy clearing, golden light illuminating the windows, like a doll's house in a fairy-tale illustration. Darcy Marsh wasn't an enchanted princess but she had a rare self-possession that drew him.

He parked his Tahoe on the side of the road to enter his report about the vehicle she'd seen and the possible attempted break-in at her home. He was uploading the photos he'd taken when his phone rang with a call from the sheriff's department.

Sheriff Travis Walker's voice carried the strain of a long day. "Ryder, you probably want to get over here," he said. "We've found another body."

Chapter Four

Christy O'Brien lay across the front seat of her wrecker, the front of her white parka stained crimson with blood, her hands and feet wrapped with silver duct tape. The wrecker itself was nose-down in a ditch at the far end of a gravel road on the outskirts of town, snow sifting down over it like icing drizzled on a macabre cake.

Ryder turned away, pushing aside the sickness and guilt that clawed at the back of his throat. Such emotions wouldn't do anyone any good now. "I just saw her," he said. "Less than an hour ago."

"Where?" Sheriff Travis Walker, snow collecting on the brim of his Stetson and the shoulders of his black parka, scanned the empty roadside. Travis was one of the reasons Ryder had ended up in Eagle Mountain. He had visited his friend at the Walker ranch one summer and fallen in love with the place. When an opening in this division had opened up, he had put in for it.

"I was in the grocery store parking lot," Ryder

said. "She passed me. I figured she was on a call, headed to pull someone out of a ditch."

"This probably happened not too long after that." Travis played the beam of his flashlight over the wrecker. "Maybe the killer called her, pretended his car wouldn't start—maybe a dead battery. When she gets out of the wrecker to take a look, he overpowers her, tapes her up, slits her throat."

"Then shoves her into the wrecker and drives it into the ditch?"

"He may not have even had to drive it," Travis said. "Just put it into gear and give it a good push in the right direction. Then he gets in his own car and drives away."

"Who called it in?" Ryder asked.

"Nobody," Travis said. "I was coming back from a call—an attempted break-in not far from here. I turned down this road, thinking the burglar might have ducked down here. When I saw the wrecker in the ditch, I knew something wasn't right."

"An attempted break-in?" Ryder asked. "Where? When?"

"Up on Pine." Travis indicated a street to the north that crossed this one. "Maybe twenty minutes ago? A guy came home from work and surprised someone trying to jimmy his lock. He thought it was a teenager. He thought he saw an Eagle Mountain High School letter jacket."

"I saw three boys in letter jackets at the grocery store just after Christy's wrecker passed me," Ryder said. "And someone tried to break into Darcy

Marsh's place this evening—I was leaving there when you called me."

Travis frowned. "I don't like to think teenagers would do something like this, but we'll check it out." He turned back toward the wrecker. "I'll talk to the people in the houses at the other end of the road, and those in this area. Maybe someone heard or saw something."

"There would be a lot of blood," Ryder said.

"More than is in the cab of the wrecker, I'm thinking. It was the same with Kelly, did you notice? She wasn't killed in that car—and it was her car."

"I did notice," Ryder said. "There was hardly any blood in the car or even on her."

"I think she was killed somewhere else and driven up there," Travis said.

"So the killer had an accomplice?" Ryder asked. "Someone who could have followed him up to the pass in another car, then taken him away?"

"Maybe," Travis said. "Or he could have walked back into town. It's only about three miles. We'll try to find out if anyone saw anything." He walked to the back of his cruiser and took out a shovel. "I don't think Christy was killed very far from here. There wasn't time. I want to see if I can find any evidence of that." He followed the fast-filling tracks of the wrecker back to the road and began to scrape lightly at the snow.

Ryder fetched his own shovel from his vehicle and tried the shoulder on the other side of the road. The work was slow and tedious as he scraped, then shone his light on the space he had uncovered. After ten minutes or so, the work paid off. "Over here," he called to Travis.

The blood glowed bright as paint against the frozen ground—great splashes of it that scarcely looked real. Travis crouched to look. "We'll get a sample, but I'm betting it's Christy's blood," he said.

"Whoever did this would have blood on his clothes, maybe in his vehicle," Ryder said.

Travis nodded. "He could have gone straight home, or to wherever he's staying, and discarded the clothes—maybe burned them in a woodstove or fireplace, if he has one. There's no one out tonight to see him, though we'll ask around." He stood. "You said you were at Darcy's place?"

"Right. When she got home tonight, there was a strange vehicle leaving. I found signs that someone tried to break in."

"What time was this?" Travis asked.

Ryder checked his notes. "Seven forty."

"The person or persons who tried to break in to Fred Starling's place might have come from Darcy's, but I don't see how they would have had time to drive from Darcy's, kill Christy, then break in to Fred's," Travis said. "We'll see what the ME gives us for time of death." He glanced down the road. "He should be here soon."

"I didn't like leaving Darcy alone out there," Ryder said. "It's kind of remote."

"I've already called in one of our reserve officers," Travis said. "I'll have him drive by Darcy's place and check on her. Why did she call you?"

"I gave her my card when we spoke earlier and told her to call if she needed anything." Ryder shifted his weight, thinking maybe it was time to change the subject. Not that he thought Travis was a stickler over jurisdiction, but he didn't think Darcy would welcome any further attention from the sheriff. "What are you doing, pulling the night shift?" he asked. "Doesn't the sheriff get any perks?"

"The new officer who's supposed to be working tonight has the flu," Travis said. He shrugged. "I figured I'd make a quick patrol, then spend the rest of the night at my desk. I have a lot of loose ends to tie up before the wedding and honeymoon."

"I hope the weather cooperates with your plans," Ryder said. "The highway department says the pass could be closed for the next two or three days—longer if this snow keeps up."

"Most of the wedding party is already here, and the ones who aren't will be coming in soon," Travis said. "My sister, Emily, pulled in this afternoon, about half an hour ahead of the closure."

He turned to gaze down the street, distracted by the headlights approaching—the medical examiner, Butch Collins, followed by the ambulance. Butch, a portly man made even larger by the ankle-length duster and long knitted scarf he wore, climbed out of his truck, old-fashioned medical bag in hand. "Two dead women in one day is a little much, don't you think, Sheriff?" He nodded to Ryder. "Is there a connection between the two?"

Ryder checked for any lurking reporters, but saw none. He nodded to the ambulance driver, who had pulled to the side of the road, steam pouring in clouds from the tailpipe of the idling vehicle. "Both women had their hands and feet bound with duct tape, and their throats slit," he said. "It looks like they weren't killed in the vehicle, but their bodies were put into the vehicles after death."

Collins nodded. "All right. I'll take a look."

Ryder and Travis moved to Travis's cruiser. "Darcy said Kelly was going shopping today," Ryder said. "She couldn't think of anyone who would want to hurt Kelly. No one had been threatening her or making her feel uneasy. You're a little more tied in with the town than I am. Do you know of anyone who might have had a disagreement with her—boyfriend, client or a competitor?"

"I didn't know her well. My parents had Kelly or Darcy out to the ranch a few times to take care of horses. I remember my mom said she liked them. I knew them well enough to wave to. I don't think she was dating anyone, though I'll ask Lacy. She keeps up with that kind of gossip more than I do." Travis's fiancée was a local woman, near Kelly's age. "I never heard anything about unhappy clients. As for competitors, there's really only Ed Nichols."

"What do you know about him?" Ryder asked.

"Darcy said he wasn't too happy about them opening up a competing practice."

"Ed's all right," Travis said. "He might have grumbled a little when the two women first arrived, but it's understandable he would feel threatened—two attractive, personable young women. I imagine it cut into his business."

"I talked to him and his wife this afternoon," Ryder said. "He seemed genuinely shaken by the news that Kelly was dead."

"It's hard to picture Ed doing something like this," Travis said. "But we'll check his alibi for the time of Christy's death."

"What about a connection between Kelly and Christy?" Ryder asked. "Were they specific targets, or random?"

"Maybe Kelly was the target and the killer went after Christy because she was the one who pulled the car with Kelly's body in it out from its hiding place?" Travis shook his head. "It's too early to make any kind of hypothesis, really."

"I've got a bad feeling about this."

"I don't like to use the words serial killer," Travis said. "But that could be what we're looking at."

"After I found Kelly's body, I was worried her murderer had gotten away before the road closed," Ryder said. "If he did, we might never find him."

"Looks like he didn't get out," Travis said. "Which could be a much bigger problem."

"I hear you," Ryder said. As long as the road

stayed blocked, the killer couldn't leave—but none of his potential victims could get very far away, either.

DARCY CONSIDERED CLOSING the clinic the next day, out of respect for Kelly. But what would she do, then, other than sit around and be sad? Work would at least provide a distraction. And the clinic had been her and Kelly's shared passion. Keeping it open seemed a better way to honor her than closing the doors.

The morning proved busy. Most of the people who had come in had heard about Kelly and were eager to share their memories of her. Darcy passed out tissues and shed a few tears of her own, but the release of admitting her grief felt good. Knowing she wasn't alone in her pain made it a tiny bit more bearable.

The office manager, Stacy, left for lunch, but Darcy stayed behind, claiming she had too much work to do. If she was being honest with herself, however, she could admit she didn't want to go out in public to face all the questions and speculation surrounding Kelly's murder, especially since one of her last patients of the day had told her the newest edition of the *Eagle Mountain Examiner* had just hit the stands, with a story about the two murders filling the front page. The editor must have stayed up late to get the breaking news in before the paper went to the printer.

Murder. The word sent a shiver through her. It still seemed so unreal. Who would want to harm Kelly? Or Christy? Darcy hardly knew the other woman, but she had seemed nice enough. Not that nice people didn't get killed, but not in places like Eagle Mountain. Maybe she was wrong to think that, but she couldn't shake her belief that this small, beautiful town was somehow immune to that kind of violence.

She was forcing herself to eat a cup of yogurt from the office refrigerator when the phone rang. She should have let it go straight to the answering service, but what if it was Ryder, with news about Kelly? Or Kelly's parents, wanting to talk?

She picked up the receiver. "Hello?"

A thin, quavering voice came over the line. "Is this the vet?" The woman—Darcy thought it was a woman—asked.

"Yes. This is Dr. Marsh. Who is this?"

"Oh, my name is Marge. Marge Latham. You don't know me. I'm in town visiting my cousin and I got trapped here by the weather. Me and my dog, Rufus. Rufus is why I'm calling."

"What's the problem with Rufus?" Darcy called up the scheduling program on the office computer as she spoke.

"He's hurt his leg," the woman said. "I don't know what's wrong with it, but he can't put any weight on it and he's in a lot of pain. It's so upsetting." Her voice broke. "He's all I have, you see, and if something happens to him, I don't know what I'd do."

"If you can bring Rufus in at three today I can see him," Darcy said. The patient before that was routine vaccinations, so that shouldn't take too long. The patient after might have to wait a little, but most people understood about emergencies.

"I was hoping you could come here," Marge said. "He's such a big dog—he weighs over a hundred pounds. I can't possibly lift him to get him into the car."

"What kind of dog is Rufus?" Darcy asked.

"He's a mastiff. Such a sweet boy, but moving him is a problem for me. I was told you do house calls."

"Only for large animals," Darcy said. "Horses and cows." And llamas and goats and one time, a pig. But they had to draw the line somewhere. Most dogs were used to riding in the car and would climb in willingly—even mastiffs.

"Well, Rufus is as big as a small horse," Marge said.

"Is there anyone who can help you get him to the office?" Darcy asked. "Maybe your sister or a nephew—"

"No, dear, that isn't possible. Won't you please come? The other vet already said no and I don't know what I'll do. He's all I have." She choked back a sob and Darcy's stomach clenched. She couldn't let an animal suffer—or risk this old woman hurting herself trying to handle the dog by herself.

"I could stop by after work tonight," she said. "But we don't close until six today, so it would be after that."

"That would be wonderful. Thank you so much."

The address the woman rattled off didn't sound familiar to Darcy, but that wasn't unusual. Four months was hardly enough time to learn the maze of gravel roads and private streets that crisscrossed the county. "Let me have your number, in case I'm running late," Darcy said.

"Oh, that would be my sister's number. Let me see. What is that?" The sounds of shuffling, then Marge slowly read off a ten-digit number. "Thank you again, dear. And Rufus thanks you, too."

Darcy hung up the phone and wrote the woman's information at the bottom of the schedule, and stuffed the notes she had taken into her purse.

Five and a half hours later, Darcy drove slowly down Silverthorne Road, leaning forward and straining her eyes in the fading light, searching for the address Marge had given her. But the numbers weren't adding up. She spotted 2212 and 2264 and 2263, but no 2237. Had Marge gotten it wrong?

Darcy slowed at each driveway to peer up the dark path, but usually she couldn't even make out a house, as the drive invariably turned into a thick tunnel of trees. Growing exasperated, she pulled to the side of the road and took out her phone and punched in the number Marge had given her. A harsh tone made her pull the phone from her ear, and a mechanical voice informed her that the number she had dialed was no longer in service or had been changed.

Darcy double-checked the number, but she had it right. And she was sure she hadn't written it down wrong. So was Marge completely confused, or was something else going on? "I should have asked her sister's name," Darcy muttered. "Then maybe I could have looked up her address."

Or maybe there wasn't a sister. A cold that had

nothing to do with the winter weather began to creep over her. No. She pushed the thought away. There was no reason to turn this into something sinister. It was simply a matter of a confused old woman, a stranger in town, getting mixed up about the address. Darcy would go into town and stop by the sheriff's department. The officers there knew the county front to back. They might have an idea where to find a visitor with an injured mastiff and her sister.

With shaking hands, Darcy put the car in gear and eased on to the road once more, tires crunching on the packed snow, even as more of the white stuff sifted down. As soon as she found a place to turn around, she would. But houses were far apart out here, and the narrow driveways difficult to see in the darkness. She missed the first drive, but was able to pull into the next, and carefully backed out again and prepared to return to town.

She had just shifted the Subaru into Drive when lights blinded her. A car or truck, its headlights on bright, was speeding toward her. She put up one hand to shield her eyes, and used the other hand to flash her high beams. Whoever was in that vehicle was driving much too fast, and didn't he realize he was blinding her?

She eased over closer to the side of the road, annoyance building, but irritation gave way to fear as she realized the other car wasn't slowing, and it wasn't moving over. She slammed her hand into the horn, the strident blare almost blocking the sound of the racing engine, but still, the oncoming vehicle didn't slow or veer away.

Panic climbed her throat and she scarcely had time to brace herself before the other car hit her, driving her car into the ditch and engulfing her in darkness.

Chapter Five

Travis had offered one of the sheriff's department conference rooms as a temporary situation room for the investigation into the murders of Kelly Farrow and Christy O'Brien. Until the roads opened and Colorado State Patrol investigators could take over, Ryder would work with Travis and his officers.

On Wednesday evening, he met with Travis and deputies Dwight Prentice and Gage Walker, to review what they knew so far. Travis yielded the whiteboard to Ryder and took a seat at the conference table with his officers.

"Our interviews with neighbors and our calls for information from anyone who might have seen anything in the vicinity of both crime scenes have turned up nothing useful," Ryder began. He had spent part of the day talking to people in houses and businesses near where the crimes had taken place. "That's not terribly surprising, considering both murders took place in isolated areas, during bad weather."

"That could mean the murderer is familiar with

this area," Dwight said. "He knows the places he's least likely to be seen."

Ryder wrote this point on the whiteboard.

"It's a rural area, so isolated places aren't hard to find," Gage said.

"Point taken," Ryder said, and made a note. He moved on to the next item on his list. "We didn't find any fingerprints on either of the vehicles involved."

"Right. But everyone wears gloves in winter," Dwight said.

"And even dumb criminals have seen enough movies or television to know to wear gloves," Gage said.

"What about the tire impressions?" Ryder asked. "There was a lot of fresh snow at both scenes."

"We don't have a tire impression expert in the department," Travis said. "But we know how to take castings and photographs and we've compared them to databases online."

Dwight flipped pages in a file and pulled out a single sheet. "Best match is a standard winter tire that runs on half the vehicles in the county," he said. "We've even got them on one of the sheriff's department cruisers."

"And the snow was so fresh and dry that the impressions we got weren't good enough to reveal any unusual characteristics," Travis said.

Ryder glanced down at the legal pad in his hand for the next item on his list. "We have blood samples, but no way to send them for matching until the roads open up," he said.

"Could be tomorrow, could be next week," Gage

said. "One weather station says the weather is going to clear and the other says another storm system is on the way."

Impatient as the news made him, Ryder knew there was no point getting stressed about something he couldn't control. "What about the duct tape?" He looked at the three at the table.

"Maybe a fancy state lab would come up with something more," Gage said. "But as far as we could tell, it's the standard stuff pretty much everybody has a roll of."

Ryder nodded. He hadn't expected anything there, but he liked to check everything off his list. "Have we found any links between Kelly and Christy?" he asked.

"Christy had a cat," Gage said. "Kelly saw it one time, for a checkup."

"When was that?" Ryder asked.

"Three months ago," Gage said.

"Anything else?" Ryder asked. "Did they socialize together? Belong to the same groups or organizations?"

The other three men shook their heads. "I questioned Christy's mom and dad about who she dated," Gage said. "I thought I might be able to match her list to a list of who Kelly went out with. I mean, it's a small town. There are only so many match-ups. But I struck out there."

"How so?" Ryder asked.

"Christy is engaged to a welder over in Delta," Gage said. "They've been seeing each other for three years. I talked to him on the phone. He's pretty torn up about this—and he couldn't have gotten here last night, anyway, since the road was still blocked."

"What about Kelly's dating history?" Ryder asked. "Anything raise any questions there?"

Gage shook his head. "That was harder to pull together, but Darcy gave me some names. One of them moved away two months ago. The other two have alibis that check out."

Ryder had to stop himself from asking how Darcy was doing. She obviously hadn't had any more trouble from whoever had tried to break into her place. He might find an excuse to stop by there later, just to make sure.

"Ed Nichols was home with his wife, watching TV last night when Christy was killed," Travis said.

"I'm guessing he wasn't too happy to see you," Ryder said, recalling his own less-than-warm reception in the Nicholses' home.

"Ed was okay, but his wife is furious," Travis said. "But I think they were telling the truth. There was six inches of snow in the driveway when I pulled in last night, and no sign that Ed's truck or her car had moved in the last few hours."

Ryder consulted his notes again, but he had reached the end of his list. "What else do we have?" he asked.

"I questioned some of the high school kids this afternoon," Gage said. "And I talked to the teachers. No one knew anything about any guys in letter jackets who might have been out last night, trying to break into homes. I got the impression some of the students might not have been telling me everything they knew, but it's hard to see a connection between attempted break-ins and these murders."

"If students were in that area last night, they might have seen the killer, or his vehicle," Travis said. "I want to find and talk to them."

"Anything else?" Ryder asked.

"The ME says both women had their throats cut with a smooth-bladed, sharp knife," Travis said. "No defensive wounds, although Christy had some bruising, indicating she might have thrashed around quite a bit after the killer taped her hands and feet."

"So the murderer was able to surprise the women and bind them before they fought much," Dwight said.

"Might have been two men," Gage said. "No woman is going to lie still while you tape her up like that."

"One really strong man might be able to subdue a frightened woman," Travis said.

"Or maybe they were drugged," Dwight said. "A quick jab with a hypodermic needle, or chloroform on a rag or something."

Ryder frowned. "I don't think there are any facilities here to test that," he said. "And even if we collect DNA from the bodies, we don't have any way of testing or matching it here."

"Right," Travis said. "We'll have to hold the bodies at the funeral home until the roads open."

Meanwhile, whoever did this was running free to

kill again. "I spoke with the friends and family of both women," Ryder said. "None of them were aware of anyone who had made threats or otherwise bothered Kelly or Christy."

"There was no sexual assault," Travis said. "Whoever did this was quick. He killed them and got out of there. No lingering."

"We can't say they weren't targeted killings, but right now it feels random," Ryder said.

"Thrill killings," Gage said. "He did it because he could get away with it."

"If that's the case, he's likely to kill again," Travis said.

The others nodded, expressions sober. Ryder's stomach churned. He felt he ought to be out doing something to stop the murderer, but what?

Travis's phone buzzed and he answered it. "Sheriff Walker." He stilled, listening. "When? Where? Tell the officer we'll be right there."

He ended the call and looked to the others. "A 911 call just came in from Darcy Marsh. Someone attacked her tonight—ran her car off the road."

"Darcy! Darcy! Wake up, honey." Darcy struggled out of a confused daze, wincing at the light blinding her. She moaned, and the light shifted away. "Darcy, look at me."

She forced herself to look into the calm face of a middle-age man who spoke with authority. "What happened?" Darcy managed, forcing the words out, the effort of speaking exhausting her.

"You were in a wreck. I'm Emmett Baxter with Eagle Mountain EMS. Can you tell me what hurts?"

"Everything," Darcy said, and closed her eyes again. She had a vague recollection of dialing 911 earlier, but her memories since then were a jumbled mess.

"Don't go to sleep now," Emmett said. "Open your eyes. Can you move your feet for me?"

Darcy tried to ignore him, then the sharp odor of ammonia stung her nose and her eyes popped open. "That's better." Emmett smiled. "Now, tell me your name."

"Darcy Marsh."

He asked a few more questions she recognized as an attempt to assess her mental awareness — her address, birthdate, telephone number and the date.

"Now try to move your feet for me," he said.

Darcy moved her feet, then her hands. The fog that had filled her head had cleared. She took stock of her surroundings. She was in her car, white powder coating most of the interior, the deflated airbag spilling out of the steering wheel like a grotesque tongue. "My face hurts," she said.

"You're going to have a couple of black eyes and some bruises," Emmett said. He shone a light into each eye. "Does anything else hurt? Any back or neck pain, or difficulty breathing?"

She shook her head. "No."

He released the catch of Darcy's seat belt. "I'm going to fit you with a cervical collar just in case." He stripped the plastic wrapping from the padded collar and fit it to her neck, the Velcro loud in her ears. "How do you feel about getting out of the car and walking over to the ambulance?" he asked. "I'll help."

"Okay." Carefully, she swung her legs over to the side of the car, Emmett's arm securely around her. They both froze as the bright beams of oncoming headlights blinded them.

"I'm not sure why the state patrol is here," Emmett said.

Ryder, a powerful figure in his sharp khaki and blue, emerged from the cruiser and strode toward the car. His gaze swept over the damaged vehicle and came to rest on Darcy's face. The tenderness in that gaze made her insides feel wobbly, and tears threatened. "Darcy, are you okay?" he asked.

She clamped her lips together to hold back a sob and managed, almost grateful for the pain the movement caused. At least it distracted her from this terrible need to throw her arms around him and weep.

"We're just going to get her over to the ambulance where we can get a better look at her," Emmett said.

"Let me help." Not waiting for a response, Ryder leaned down and all but lifted her out of the car. He propped her up beside him and walked her to the back of the ambulance, then stepped aside while Emmett and a female EMT looked her over.

"You're going to be pretty sore tomorrow," Emmett pronounced when they were done. "But there's no swelling or indication that anything is broken and

I can't find any sign of internal damage. How do you feel? Any nausea or pain?"

"I'm a little achy and still shaken up," Darcy said. "But I don't think I'm seriously injured."

"With the highway still closed, we can't transport you to the hospital, but I'd recommend a visit to the clinic in town. They can do X-rays and maybe keep you overnight for observation."

"No, I really don't think that's necessary," she said. "I think I just had the wind knocked out of me. If I start to feel worse, I promise I'll see a doctor."

Emmett nodded. "Don't hesitate to call us if that changes or you have any questions." He glanced over his shoulder at Ryder, who stood, arms folded across his chest, gaze fixed on Darcy. "Your turn."

For the first time Darcy realized there were other people at the scene—Travis and another man in a sheriff's department uniform, and several people in jeans and parkas who might have been neighbors. Ryder sat beside her on the back bumper of the ambulance while Travis came to stand beside them. "What happened?" he asked.

She took a deep breath, buying time to organize her thoughts. "I got a call at lunchtime today," she said. "When I was alone in the office. A woman who said her name was Marge asked me if I could make a house call to look at her mastiff who had hurt his leg. She said she was staying with her sister and had been trapped by the weather. She gave me an address on this street, but I couldn't find the number. I tried to call her, but the phone number she had given me wasn't a working number. I turned around and started to head back toward town when this vehicle blinded me with its headlights and ran into me." She put a hand to her head, wincing. "I must have blacked out for a minute, then I guess I came to and called for help, then passed out again. I didn't come to completely until the ambulance was here."

"A man backing out of his driveway saw the accident and called 911, too," Travis said. "He didn't get a good look at the vehicle that hit you, though he thinks it was a truck. He said it drove off after it put your car in the ditch."

Darcy looked toward her car, which was canted to one side in a snowbank. "He hit me almost head-on," she said. "My car's probably ruined."

"Had you ever heard from this Marge person before?" Ryder asked.

"No. She said her name was Marge Latham. I didn't think to ask for her sister's name."

"What was the address she gave you?" Travis asked.

"Two two three seven Silverthorne Road," Darcy said. "She said her dog's name was Rufus. She sounded really old, and said he was a mastiff, and too big for her to lift."

"You say you were alone in the office when the call came in?" Ryder asked.

"Yes. I had just sent Stacy to lunch. I stayed in to catch up on some work."

"So anyone watching the office would have known you were alone," Ryder said.

She stared at him. "Why do you think someone was watching the office? Why would they do that?"

His grim expression sent a shiver of fear through her. "I think someone made that call to get you out here, so they could run you off the road," he said. "The neighbor backing out of his driveway probably scared him off."

She hugged her arms across her stomach, fighting nausea. "Do you think it's the same person who killed Kelly and Christy?"

Ryder and Travis exchanged a look. "Is there anyone you can stay with for a while?" Ryder asked.

"No," she said. If Kelly was still alive, Darcy might have stayed with her, but that wasn't possible now. And the thought of leaving her little home was wrenching. "I don't want to leave the cats. I'll be fine."

A young uniformed officer approached. "The wrecker is here," he said. "Where do you want the car towed?"

All three men looked at Darcy. "Oh. Is there a mechanic in town?"

"There's O'Brien's," the officer said. "That's where the wrecker's from."

"Then I guess tow it there," she said.

"I'll drive you home," Ryder said.

There was no point in refusing—she didn't have any other way to get home, and she could see he wasn't going to take no for an answer. He helped her to his Tahoe and she climbed in. They rode in silence; she was still numb from everything that had happened. At the house he took the keys from her and opened the door, then checked through the house—which took all of a minute—the cats observing him from their perches on the stairs to the loft.

Darcy unbuttoned her coat and Ryder returned to her side to help her out of it. He draped it on the hook by the door, then hung his leather patrolman's jacket beside it. "Sit, and I'll make you some tea," he said.

She started to protest that he didn't have to wait on her. He didn't have to stay and look after her. She wanted to be alone. Instead, she surrendered to her wobbly knees and shakier emotions and slid onto the bench seat at the little table and watched while Ryder familiarized himself with her galley kitchen. Within minutes he had a kettle heating on the stove and was opening a can of soup.

"You don't have to stay," she said.

"No." He took two bowls from a cabinet and set them on the counter. "You've had a fright. I figured you could use some company." His eyes met hers. "And I'd rather stay here than go home to my empty place and worry about you out here alone."

"I'll be fine," she said. "I can see anyone coming, the locks are good and I have my gun and my phone."

"Use the phone first."

"Of course." She shivered. She had only ever fired the gun at the range. Could she really use it on a person? Maybe. If her life depended on it. "But I think I'm safe here." If she kept repeating the words, she might make them true.

"You should install an alarm system," he said.

"That's a great idea. But the nearest alarm company is in Junction—on the other side of Dixon Pass." Not accessible until the road reopened.

He stirred the soup, the rhythmic sound calming. Elinor the cat settled onto the bench next to Darcy, purring. She stroked the cat and tried to soak in all this soothing comfort. "Why is this happening?" she asked.

"Have you thought of anything at all that's happened the past few weeks that's been out of the ordinary?" he asked. "A client who was difficult, a man who leered at you in the grocery store—anything at all?"

"No."

"And no one who might have a grudge against you, or resentment—other than the other vet."

She hesitated. There was Ken, but he didn't really hate her. He had only had his feelings hurt because she had refused to continue dating him. But she had never felt threatened by him. Ryder turned toward her. "Who are you thinking of?"

She sighed. "There was a guy I went out with a few times—Ken Rutledge. He lives next door to Kelly, in the other half of the duplex. I thought he was getting too serious too quickly, so I broke things off. He wasn't happy about it, but I can't believe he would *kill* anyone. I mean, he's just not the violent type." She would have said the same about the man who raped her, too, though.

"I'll have a talk with him," Ryder said. He poured soup into the two bowls and brought them to the table. "I won't tell him you said anything. If he was Kelly's neighbor, I need to talk to him, anyway."

"Thank you." She leaned over the bowl of soup and the smell hit her, making her mouth water. Suddenly, she was ravenous. She tried not to look like a pig, but she inhaled the soup and drained the cup of tea, then sat back. "I feel much better now," she said.

Ryder smiled. His eyes crinkled at the corners when he did so. A shadow of beard darkened his chin and cheeks, giving him a rakish look. "You're not as pale," he said. "Though I bet you're going to be pretty sore tomorrow."

"But I'll heal," she said. "I'm not so sure about my car. And how am I going to get to work?" Her predicament had just sunk in. "It's not as if Eagle Mountain has a car rental agency."

"I'm pretty sure Bud O'Brien keeps a couple of loaner vehicles for customers," Ryder said.

"I hate to bother him," Darcy said. "The man just lost his daughter." Her stomach clenched, thinking of the woman who had been murdered.

"The people who work for him will be there," Ryder said. "Too many people would be left stranded in this weather if they closed their doors. Call them in the morning and someone will work something out for you. If not, give me a call and I'll put out some feelers."

"Thanks."

Ryder insisted on staying to help clean up and do the dishes. They worked side by side in her tiny kitchen. He seemed too large for the compact space, and yet comfortable in it, as well. Finally, when the last dish was returned to its place in her cabinets, he slipped on his jacket.

"You're sure you'll be comfortable here by yourself?" he asked.

He was standing very close to her so that she was very aware of his size and strength. She wasn't exactly uncomfortable, but her heart beat a little too fast, and she had trouble controlling her breathing.

"Darcy?"

He was looking at her, waiting on an answer. She cleared her throat. "I'll keep my phone with me and I'll call 911 if I see or hear anything suspicious."

"Call me, too," he said. "I'm going to have the phone company try to track the number the call came from, but if you hear from Marge again, you'll let me know."

It wasn't a request—more of an order. "I will," she said. "Part of me still hopes it was a mistake— a confused woman who wasn't familiar with the area gave me the wrong address and phone number."

"It would be nice if that were the case," he said. "But I think it's better to act as if it was a genuine threat and be prepared for it to happen again."

His words sent a shudder through her, but she braced herself against it and met his gaze. "I'll be careful," she said.

He rested his hand lightly on her shoulder. "I'm not trying to frighten you," he said.

She wanted to lean into him, to rest her cheek against his hand like a cat. Instead, she made herself stand still and smile, though the expression felt weak. "I know. I'm already frightened, but I won't let the fear defeat me."

"That's the attitude." He bent and kissed her cheek, the brush of his lips sending a jolt of awareness through her. She reached up to pull him to her, but he had already turned away. She leaned in the open doorway.

He strode to his car, his boots crunching in the snow. He lifted his hand in a wave as he climbed into the Tahoe, then he was gone. And still she stood, with the door wide open. But she didn't feel the cold, still warmed by that brief kiss.

Chapter Six

Ryder's first impression of Ken Rutledge was an overgrown boy. On a day when the temperatures hovered in the twenties, Rutledge wore baggy cargo shorts and a striped sweater, and the sullen expression of a teen who had been forced to interact with dull relatives. "You're that cop who's investigating Kelly's murder," he said by way of greeting when he opened the door to Ryder.

"Ryder Stewart." Ryder didn't offer his hand—he had the impression Rutledge wouldn't have taken it. "I need to ask you some questions."

"You'd better come in." Rutledge moved out of the doorway and into a cluttered living room. A guitar and two pairs of skis leaned against one wall, while a large-screen TV and a video gaming console occupied most of another. Rutledge clearly liked his toys.

Rutledge leaned against the door frame of the entrance to the kitchen, arms folded across his chest. "What do you want to know?" he asked.

"How well did you know Kelly Farrow?" Ryder asked.

"Pretty well. I mean, we lived right next to each other. We were friends."

"Did you ever date her?"

Rutledge grinned. "She flirted with me. I think she would have gone out with me if I'd asked, but she wasn't my type."

Ryder wondered if this meant he'd asked her out, but Kelly had turned him down. "What is your type?"

"I like a woman who's a little quieter. Petite. Kelly had too much of a mouth on her."

Quiet and petite—like Darcy. Ryder took out his notebook and pen—more to have something to do with his hands than to make notes. He wasn't likely to forget anything this guy said. "You dated Darcy Marsh," he said.

Rutledge shifted, uncrossing his arms and tucking his thumbs in the front pockets of the cargo shorts. "We went out a few times."

"She says you weren't too happy when she broke it off."

"Yeah, well, she would say that, wouldn't she?"

"What do you mean?"

"Women always try to make themselves look like the victim."

"So what did happen between you two?" Ryder asked.

"I was really busy—I teach school and coach basketball. Darcy was a little too needy. I didn't give her the attention she wanted." He shrugged. "I let her down easy but I guess I hurt her feelings, anyway."

Ryder pretended to consult his notebook. "Where were you last night about six thirty?" he asked.

"Why? Did they find another body?"

"Answer the question, please."

"Yeah, sure. Let's see—there was a game at the high school. The varsity team—I coach JV—but I was there to watch."

Ryder made a note of this. It ought to be easy enough to check. "What about Tuesday night?" he asked.

"I was home, playing an online game with a couple of friends."

"I'll need their names and contact information."

"Sure. I can give that to you." He moved to a laptop that was open on a table by the sofa and manipulated a mouse. While he made notes on a sheet of paper torn from a spiral notebook, Ryder looked around the room. There were no photographs, and the only artwork on the wall was a framed poster from a music festival in a nearby town.

"Here you go." Rutledge handed Ryder the piece of paper. "And since I know you're going to ask anyway, the day Kelly was killed, I was teaching school. That'll be easy for you to check."

Ryder folded the paper and tucked it into the back of his notebook. "Do you have any idea who might have wanted to kill Kelly Farrow?" he asked. "Did she ever mention anyone who had threatened her, or did you ever see anyone suspicious near the house?"

Ken shook his head. "It could have been anybody, really," he said.

Most people said things like "everybody liked Kelly" or "she never made an enemy." "Why do you say that?" Ryder asked.

"Like I said, she had a mouth on her. And she dated lots of men—though none for very long. Maybe she said the wrong thing to one of them."

"And you think that would justify killing her?"

Ken took a step back. "No, man. I'm just saying, if the wrong guy had a hair trigger—it might be enough to make him snap. There are a lot of sick people in this world."

Ryder put away the notebook and took out one of his cards. "Call me if you think of anything," he said. Though Rutledge's alibis sounded solid enough, he couldn't shake the feeling the man was hiding something. Ryder would be keeping an eye on him.

At seven thirty Thursday morning a mechanic from O'Brien's Garage delivered a battered pickup truck in several shades of green and gray to Darcy's door. "She looks like crap, but she runs good," the young man said as he handed over the keys. He rode off with the friend who had followed him to her place, and Darcy hoisted herself up into the vehicle, wishing for a step stool, it was so high off the ground. She felt tiny in the front seat—even the steering wheel felt too big for her hands. But as promised, the truck ran smoothly and carried her safely into town.

She had discarded the cervical collar that morning. While much of her was sore, none of the aches and pains felt serious. Her patients might all have fur or feathers, but she considered herself competent to assess her own injuries.

She stopped by Eagle Mountain Grocery, hoping the store would be mostly empty this time of morning. All she needed was a deli sandwich, since she planned to eat lunch at her desk again. She had layered on makeup in an attempt to hide the worst of the bruising, but she was sure she faced a day full of explaining what had happened to her.

As hoped, the store was mostly empty when she arrived. She hurried to the deli and ordered a turkey sandwich on cranberry bread, and debated adding a cookie while the clerk filled her order. A few more minutes and she'd be safely out of here.

"Darcy Marsh, you've got a lot of nerve!"

The strident voice rang through the store like a crack of thunder. Darcy turned to see Sharon Nichols steering her grocery cart toward her. For a tense moment Darcy thought Sharon intended to run her over. She had a flash of herself, pinned to the glass-fronted deli case by the cart.

But Sharon stopped a few inches short of hitting Darcy. "Haven't you done enough to hurt us?" she demanded, lines etched deeper in her face than Darcy remembered.

"I don't know what you're talking about." Darcy spoke softly, hoping Sharon would lower her voice, as well. As it was, the two workers in the deli had both turned to stare.

"You complained about my husband to that cop and now he won't leave us alone." Sharon leaned closer, but didn't lower her voice. "He had the nerve to suggest Ed murdered those girls. Ed—who wouldn't hurt a fly! Why do you hate us so much?"

Darcy took a step back, desperately wanting to get away from Sharon and the angry words, which battered her like a club. "I don't hate you," she said. "And I never suggested Ed killed anyone. I don't believe that."

"You should go back to wherever you're from and leave us alone. Ed has lived here all his life. He had a good business, taking care of the animals in this county, then you and your friend had to move in and try to take over."

"We didn't try to take over. There's room enough in Eagle Mountain for all of us."

"That's a lie and you know it!" Sharon inched closer until the end of her cart pressed against Darcy's hips. "You came in with your fancy new office and pretty faces, undercutting us, trying to put us out of business."

"That's not true." If anything, the fees she and Kelly charged were higher than Ed's, but there was no use pointing that out to Sharon. Darcy glanced around. Two women peered from the end of one aisle, and one of the checkout people and a stocker had gathered to watch, as well. "I think you should go," she said softly.

"You won't run us out of town," Sharon said, tears streaming down her face. "You won't. We'll force you to leave first."

She turned and, seeing her chance, Darcy fled.

She fumbled the keys into the ignition of the truck and drove out of the lot, scarcely seeing her surroundings, her mind too full of the image of Sharon Nichols's furious face.

Her final words, about making Darcy leave town, left a sick feeling in the pit of Darcy's stomach. She had never seen anyone so angry. Was Ed that angry, too? Were the Nicholses angry enough to kill?

RYDER STEPPED INTO the clinic and was greeted by furious barking from a small white terrier, who strained on the end of its leash. "I'm sorry about that." A middle-age woman with red curly hair scooped up the barking dog. "He thinks he has to protect me from everyone."

"Hello, Officer." The receptionist, a blue-eyed blonde with long, silver-painted fingernails, greeted him from behind the front counter. "What can I do for you?"

"I'd like a word with Darcy, if she's free."

"Wait just a few minutes."

He took a seat. The terrier glared at him from the redhead's lap. The office smelled of disinfectant. A brochure rack on the wall offered information on various ailments from arthritis to kennel cough, and a locked cabinet displayed a variety of cat and dog food and treats.

The door to the back office opened and a gray-haired couple emerged, the man toting a cat carrier. Darcy followed them out. "Bring her back on Tuesday and we'll remove the bandage," Darcy said.

"And don't let her near any more mousetraps." She looked over Ryder's shoulder and sent him a questioning look.

He stood and as the couple moved to the front desk to pay, he slipped through the door and followed her into a small exam room where she sprayed the exam table with disinfectant and began to wipe it down. "Stacy said you wanted to talk to me," she said.

He shut the door to the room behind him. "Just to tell you that I talked to Ken Rutledge and his alibis for last night, and the times of the murders check out." Several people remembered seeing Ken at the basketball game, his online buddies had vouched for the times he had been involved in their game and he had had a full load of classes the day Kelly was murdered, including lunchroom and bus duty.

"I'm glad to hear it." She all but sagged with relief. "I hated to think I'd misjudged him so badly—that he was capable of something like that."

"He had a different story about your relationship, though," Ryder said.

"Oh?" She went back to wiping down the table and counters.

"He says he broke it off because you were too clingy."

She let out a bark of laughter. "That's not what happened, but if it makes him feel better to say so, it doesn't make any difference to me."

"He also said Kelly flirted with him, but she wasn't his type."

"Oh, please. Kelly was gorgeous. She was nice to everyone, which I guess some men take as flirting, but she wasn't interested in Ken." She tucked the bottle of disinfectant back in a cabinet over the sink and dropped a handful of used paper towels in the trash can by the door. "To tell you the truth, I think she introduced him to me as a way to get him off her back."

"So he may be a jerk, but I don't think he's the person who's harassing you." He leaned against the end of the counter. "Have you heard any more from Marge?"

"No. And I doubt I will."

"I checked with Ed Nichols. He says he never got a call from a woman about a large dog that needed a house call."

A shadow passed over her face as if she was in pain. "What is it?" Ryder asked. "What's wrong?"

She glanced over his shoulder as if making sure the door was still closed. "I ran into Sharon Nichols at the grocery store this morning," she said. "She cornered me and demanded to know why I was trying to ruin her husband's life. She was so furious, she was almost…unhinged."

Ryder tensed. "Did she threaten you?"

"Not exactly."

"What did she say—exactly?"

"She said I wouldn't run them out of town—that they would make me leave first."

"She didn't elaborate?"

"No. And I really think she was just talking. She was so upset."

"I'll have a word with her."

"No." She grabbed his arm. "Please. You'll only make things worse."

His first inclination was to deny this. If the Nicholses had any intention of harming Darcy, he wanted to make it clear he would see they were punished, swiftly and harshly.

But the pleading look in Darcy's eyes forced him to calm down. "I won't say anything to them," he said. "But I will keep an eye on them."

She took her hand from his arm. He wanted to pull it back—to pull her close and comfort her. Last night he had kissed her cheek on impulse, but he had wanted to kiss her lips. Would she have pushed him away if he tried?

"I need to get back to work," she said, glancing toward the door again.

"Just one more question," he said. "Though you may not like it."

"Oh?"

"What happened with the man who raped you?"

She hadn't expected that, he could tell. "If he's not in prison, I think it would be worth tracking him down," he said. "Just to make sure he isn't in Rayford County."

She nodded. "He was caught. I testified at the trial. I think he's still in prison."

"What was his name?"

"Jay Leverett. You don't think he's come after me again—not here?" Her skin had turned a shade paler.

"I'm just going to check."

She nodded. "This whole thing scares me. But I can't let that stop me from living my life."

"I don't like you out there at that little house by yourself." He'd meant to keep his fears to himself, but suddenly couldn't.

"It's my home. And my cats' home." She frowned. "Ken asked me to move in with him. I told him no way."

If Ryder asked her to move in with him, would she lump him in the same category as Ken? "You could move into Kelly's place," he said. "It's right in town, with more people around."

"No. I can't make you understand, but it's important to me to be strong enough to stay put. One thing I learned after I was raped was that fear was my worst enemy. Let me put it this way—if you were the one being threatened, would you move out of your home?"

"Probably not." He wanted to argue that he was a trained professional—but that wasn't what she wanted to hear. "I'll be keeping an eye on you," he said. "And keep your phone charged and with you at all times, with my number on speed dial. Call 911 first, then call me."

"I will. And thank you." She reached past him for the doorknob. "Now I have to get back to my patients."

The terrier growled at him as he passed. He ignored the dog and went back outside. Snow swirled around him in big white flakes. The sun that had shone earlier had disappeared and there was already an inch of snow on his Tahoe. The city's one snowplow trundled past him as he waited to turn onto Main Street. From the looks of things, the highway wouldn't be opening back up today. Was the killer getting antsy, looking for his next victim? If he was the person who went after Darcy last night, he had failed. How long would he wait before trying again?

Chapter Seven

Friday afternoon Darcy watched the young woman lead the horse the length of the barn and back and nodded. "I think she's more comfortable with the leg wrapped, don't you?" she said.

"Yes, I do." Emily Walker, younger sister to Travis and Gage Walker, brushed back a sweep of long, dark hair and smiled at Darcy. "Thanks so much for coming out here to look at her." She rubbed the horse's nose. "I've only ridden her once since I got here and she was fine then. I couldn't believe it this morning when I came out and found she'd gone lame."

"Keep the wrapping on, let her rest and give her the anti-inflammatories I prescribed," Darcy said. "If she's not better in a couple of days, call me and we can do some more extensive testing, but I think she'll be okay."

"I hope so." Emily gave the horse another pat, then both women exited the stall. "Thanks again for driving out here. I wasn't really looking forward to pulling a horse trailer on these snowy roads."

"I take it you're here for the wedding?" Darcy asked.

"It's my winter break, so I'd probably be here, anyway, but of course I'm staying over for the wedding." Emily grinned. "It's going to be so beautiful. I adore Lacy and though my big brother likes to play it all serious and unemotional, I can tell he's over the moon in love. I'm so happy for them both."

"You're from Denver?" Darcy asked.

"Fort Collins. I'm in grad school at Colorado State University."

"That's where I went to school," Darcy said.

"I love it there," Emily said. She stretched her arms over her head. "But I can't tell you how great it is not to have to think about classes and data analysis and lab reports and all of that for a few weeks. I'm determined to make the most of my time at home, snow or no snow." She put a hand on Darcy's arm. "What are you doing tomorrow?"

"I have office hours until noon." With Kelly gone, she was working six days a week—six long days, since she was handling all the office visits as well as house calls. She had rearranged her schedule this afternoon in order to make this call, but she had a full slate of patients for the rest of the afternoon. She hadn't had time to think much about how she was going to manage to keep up with such a schedule.

"Come here for the afternoon," Emily said. "I'm hosting a snowshoe scavenger hunt for the wedding party and any other young people I can get up here. We might all be trapped by the snow, but that doesn't mean we can't enjoy it."

Kelly would have jumped at that kind of invitation—she adored parties and meeting new people. Darcy, on the other hand, had been looking forward to an afternoon curled up on the sofa with the cats around her and a good book. "Oh, thanks so much," she said. "But I don't think I'll be able to make it. Since my partner died I'm pretty much buried under work." Not a lie.

Emily looked as disappointed as a child who had been told she couldn't have a puppy. "I was so sorry to hear about Kelly." She squeezed Darcy's arm. "If you change your mind, come anyway. The more the merrier."

They emerged from the barn and Darcy was startled to see Ryder striding toward them. Dressed in his uniform with the black leather coat, he somehow didn't look all that out of place in the corral. "Hello, Emily, Darcy." He nodded to them. "Is everything all right?"

"It is now," Emily said. "Darcy has taken very good care of my favorite mare." She touched Darcy's arm. "Darcy, do you know Ryder Stewart? He's one of Travis's groomsmen."

"We know each other," Ryder said. A little current of heat ran through Darcy as his eyes met hers.

"If you're looking for Travis, he went somewhere with Dad," Emily said. "But they should be back pretty soon for supper. Our cook, Rainey, doesn't like it if people are late for meals, and Dad doesn't like to cross her."

"I'll catch him later," Ryder said. "It's not that important."

"Well, I'm glad you stopped by, anyway," Emily said. "You've saved me a phone call. I'm having a get-together for the wedding party and friends tomorrow afternoon—a snowshoe scavenger hunt." She turned to Darcy. "I'm trying to talk Darcy into coming, too."

"You should come," Ryder said. "It'll be good to be around other people."

She heard the unspoken message beneath his words: no one is going to bother you with half a dozen law enforcement officers around. And maybe socializing would be a good way to distract herself from worries about everything from the business to her own safety. "All right. I guess I could come."

"Wonderful," Emily said. She looked past Ryder, toward the ranch house. "My mom is waving to me—she probably needs my help with something for the wedding. With most of the wedding party staying here, you wouldn't believe how much there is to do." She waved goodbye to both of them and hurried away.

Ryder fell into step beside Darcy as they headed for the parking area near the stables where she had left the borrowed truck. Ryder laughed when he saw the green and yellow monster. "I saw this outside your office," he said. "But I had no idea it was yours."

"It's the official loaner vehicle for O'Brien's Garage," she said. "A little horrifying, but it runs well. I was glad to get anything at all, since my car will need some pretty major repairs."

"I think anyone will have a hard time running you off the road in that," Ryder said.

"Good point." The idea cheered her. She took out the keys and prepared to hoist herself into the cab, then paused. "Is everything all right?" she asked. "You aren't here to see Travis about a development in the case?"

He shook his head. "He asked me to help find extra chairs for the wedding guests and I wanted to get a look at the space where the ceremony will be. I have a couple of places that have agreed to loan some chairs, and I wanted to see what would work best."

"That's nice of you," she said.

"I'm the backup plan, really," he said. "They have a wedding planner out of Junction who's supposed to supply all that stuff, but this is in case the roads don't open in time."

"But the wedding is still over three weeks away," Darcy said. "Surely, the road will be open by then."

"Probably," he said. "But it's probably not a bad idea to plan, just in case."

"I need to go through our medical supplies and make sure we have enough of everything," she said. "I can see it will be a good idea to keep extra stock on hand in the winter." She climbed into the truck.

Ryder shut the door behind her. "Have a good evening," he said. "See you tomorrow."

"Yeah. See you tomorrow." While part of her still longed for that quiet afternoon at home, curled up with a book, she could see the sense in spending her free time around other people. That one of those people would be Ryder made the prospect all the more pleasing.

RYDER HAD JUST turned onto Main Street when his phone rang with a call from Travis. "I was just up at your place, looking at the wedding venue," Ryder said.

"I ended up getting detoured to the office," Travis said. "When you get a chance, swing by here. I've got something to show you."

"I'll be right over."

Adelaide Kinkaid, the seventy-something woman whose title Ryder didn't know, but who kept the sheriff's department running smoothly, greeted Ryder as he stepped into the station lobby. "Trooper Stewart," she said. "We're seeing so much of you lately we should make you an honorary deputy."

"Do I get to draw double pay?" Ryder asked.

Adelaide narrowed her blue eyes behind her violet-rimmed glasses. "I said *honorary*. To what do we owe the pleasure of your company today?"

"I need to speak with the sheriff."

"Of course you do. You and half the county. Don't you people know he has a wedding to prepare for?"

"I thought the bride did most of the work of weddings," Ryder said.

Adelaide sniffed. "We live in a new age, haven't you heard? Men have to pull their weight, too."

"I'm more concerned about this case than the wedding right now." Travis stood in the hallway leading to the offices. "Come on back, Ryder."

Instead of stopping at his office, Travis led the way down the hall to a conference room. He unlocked the door and ushered Ryder inside. Items, some of which Ryder recognized as being from the crime scenes, were arrayed on two long folding tables. He followed Travis around the tables. "When we originally towed Kelly's car, our intention was to secure it and leave it to the state's forensic team to process," Travis said. "After Christy's murder, with the road still closed, we felt we no longer had that luxury, so I put my team on it."

He picked up a clear plastic envelope. "They found this in Kelly's car, in the pocket on the driver's side door."

Ryder took the envelope and studied the small rectangle of white inside. A business card, with black letters: Ice Cold. "What does that mean?" he asked. "Is it supposed to be the name of a business?"

"We don't know. We didn't turn up anything in our online searches. It's not a business that we can find."

Ryder turned the packet with the card over. The back was blank, but on closer inspection, he could see that the edges of the card were slightly uneven, as if from perforations. "It looks like those blanks you can buy at office supply stores," he said. "To print your own cards at home."

"That's what we think, too," Travis said. "We think it was printed on a laser printer. The card stock is pretty common, available at a lot of places, including the office supply store here in town, though the owner doesn't show having sold any in the past month. But it could have been purchased before then."

Ryder laid the envelope back on the table. "We don't know how old it is, either," he said. "Kelly could have dropped it months ago."

"Except we found another card just like this in Christy's wrecker." Travis moved a few feet down the table and picked up a second envelope.

The card inside was identical to the one in the first envelope. A brief tremor raced up Ryder's spine. "We found it wedged between the cushions of the driver's seat," Travis said.

"Whoever left it there had to know we'd find it," Ryder said.

"I don't think he's going to stop with two murders," Travis said. "He's going to want to keep playing the game."

Ryder thought of Darcy, her car run off the road, and felt a chill. "Darcy could have been the third."

"Maybe," Travis said. "But Christy's murder, at least, feels more like a crime of opportunity. She was one of the few people out that night. The killer saw her and decided to make her his next victim."

"How do we stop him?" Ryder asked.

"I'm putting every man I can on the streets, and I'm asking the newspaper to run a story, warning everyone to be careful about stopping for strangers, suggesting they travel in pairs, things like that. I don't want to alarm people, but I don't want another victim."

"That may not be enough," Ryder said. "Some people think they're invincible—that a place like Eagle Mountain has to be safe."

"I'm trying to make it safe," Travis said. "We'll do everything we can, but we're at a disadvantage. The killer knows us and that we're looking for him." He picked up the business card again. "We'll keep trying to track down the meaning of Ice Cold."

"I'll get folks at state patrol working on it, too. We can transmit the images electronically. At least we've still got that. Did you find anything else in the vehicles that we can use?"

"Nothing. No fingerprints, no hair. Of course, with the weather, he was probably bundled up—cap, gloves, maybe even a face mask."

"Which makes it even more certain the business card was left deliberately." Anger tightened Ryder's throat. "He's treating this like some kind of game—taunting us."

"It's a game I don't intend to lose," Travis said.

Ryder nodded. But the cold knot in his stomach didn't loosen. If whoever did this killed again, someone would lose. Someone—probably a woman—

would lose her life. And the awful reality was that he and Travis and the other officers might not be able to stop it from happening.

A LATE CANCELLATION allowed Darcy to keep her pledge to take an inventory of veterinary supplies at her office Friday afternoon. To her relief, she was well stocked on most items, though her stockpile of some bandages and Elizabethan collars were running low. Fortunately, Kelly kept overflow supplies in her garage and Darcy was sure she could find what she needed there.

After closing up that evening, she drove to Kelly's duplex. She parked the truck in the driveway, then let herself in with her key and switched on the living room light. Already, the house looked vacant and neglected. Kelly's furniture and belongings were still there, of course, but dust had settled on the furniture, and the air smelled stale. She swallowed back a knot of tears and forced herself to walk straight through to the connecting door to the garage. She would get what she needed and get out, avoiding the temptation to linger and mourn her missing friend.

Darcy flipped the switch for the garage light, but only one bulb lit, providing barely enough illumination to make out the boxes stacked along the far wall. Without Kelly's car parked inside, the space looked a lot bigger. Darcy wondered what would happen to the duplex now. The rent was presumably paid up through the end of the month. Once the road opened, she assumed Kelly's parents would clean the place out.

The boxes of supplies on the back wall contained everything from paper towels and toilet paper for the veterinary office restrooms to surgical drapes and puppy pads. The friends had found a supplier who offered big discounts for buying in bulk, and had stocked up on anything nonperishable.

The bandages and plastic cones she needed were in two separate boxes on the bottom of the pile, the contents of each box noted on the outside in Kelly's neat handwriting. Darcy set her purse on the floor and started moving the top layer of boxes out of the way. At least all this activity would warm her up a little. The temperature had hovered just above freezing all day, plunging quickly as the sun set. The concrete floor of the garage might as well have been a slab of ice, radiating cold up through Darcy's feet and throughout her body.

She shifted a heavy carton labeled surgical supplies and set it on the floor with a rattling thud. The noise echoed around her and she hurried to pull out the box of bandages. She'd carry the whole thing out to the truck, then come back for the collars. She only needed a few of them, in small and medium sizes.

She picked up the bandage carton—who knew all that elastic and cloth could be so heavy?—and headed back toward the door to the kitchen. She had her foot on the bottom step when the door to the kitchen opened and the shadowy figure of a man loomed large. "What do you think you're doing?" he demanded. A flashlight blinded her, then someone knocked the box from her hand and she was falling backward, a scream caught in her throat.

Chapter Eight

Darcy tried to fight back, but the man's arms squeezed her so tightly she could scarcely breathe. She kicked out and clawed at his face, screaming and cursing. Then, as suddenly as he had grabbed her, the man let go. "Darcy! Darcy, are you okay? I had no idea it was you."

Eyes clouded with angry tears, she stared at Ken, who stood at the bottom of the steps leading into the house, a flashlight in one hand, the other held up, palm open. Darcy swiped at her eyes and straightened her clothes. "What are *you* doing here?" she asked. "And why did you attack me?"

"I didn't know it was you." He looked truly flustered. "I saw the truck in the driveway and didn't recognize it. Then I heard a noise in the garage—I thought someone was trying to rob the place."

She gathered up the scattered contents of the carton of bandages, trying to gather up a little of her dignity, as well. "Let me help you with that," Ken said, bounding down the stairs to join her. "Why are you driving that old truck?"

"My car is in the shop," she said. "Someone ran me off the road the other night."

"Oh, Darcy." He put a hand on her shoulder and looked into her eyes. "You need to be careful. Do you think it was the serial killer?"

"Serial killer?" The word struck fear into her. Could he be a serial killer if he'd only killed two people? Or had Ryder and the sheriff discovered others?

"That's what the paper is saying," Ken said. "They even printed a statement from the sheriff, telling everyone to be careful around people they don't know, and suggesting people not go out alone."

She clutched the box to her chest, pushing down the flutters of panic in her stomach. "I'm being careful," she said. So careful she was beginning to feel paranoid, scrutinizing the driver in every car she passed, looking on every new male client with suspicion.

"You shouldn't be out at your place alone," Ken said. "The offer is still open to stay with me."

"I'm fine by myself," she said. "And I couldn't leave the cats."

She pushed past him and he let her pass, but followed her into the living room. "I talked to that cop," he said. "That state trooper."

She set the box down and pulled on her gloves. "Oh?"

"He thinks I had something to do with Kelly and Christy's deaths—that I killed them, even."

She looked up, startled. "Did Ryder say that? Did he accuse you of killing them?" He had told her that

Ken's alibis for the times of the murders checked out, but maybe he had only been shielding her. Or maybe he even thought she might share information with Ken.

"He didn't have to. He grilled me—asking where was I and what was I doing when the women were killed. And he wanted to know all about my relationship with Kelly."

"He just asked you the same questions he asked everyone who knew Kelly," she said. "He wasn't accusing you of anything. And you haven't done anything wrong, so why be upset?"

"Cops can frame people for crimes, you know," he said. "Especially people they don't like, or who they want to get out of the way."

"Don't be ridiculous." She regretted the words as anger flashed in his eyes. "I mean, why would he do that?" she hastened to add. "Ryder doesn't even know you."

"He wanted to know about my relationship with you, too," Ken said. "I think he's jealous that we're friends. That we used to date."

Darcy didn't think three dates amounted to a relationship, but she wasn't going to argue the point now. "I think he's just doing his job," she said.

"I think that cop is interested in you," Ken said. "You should be careful. What if he's the serial killer?"

"Ryder?" She almost laughed, but the look on Ken's face stole away any idea that he was joking.

"It's not so far-fetched," he said. "Crooked cops

do all kinds of things. And he was the one who found Kelly's body."

"Ryder was with me when Christy was killed," she said.

Ken's eyes narrowed to slits. "What was he doing with you?" He took a step closer and she forced herself not to move away, though her heart pounded so hard it hurt.

"Someone tried to break into my house," she said. "He came to investigate."

Ken's big hand wrapped around her upper arm. "I told you it's not safe for you out there," he said, squeezing hard.

She cried out and wrenched away. She searched for her car keys and realized she had left her purse in the garage. She could do without the collars if she had to, but she couldn't go anywhere without her keys. "You can go home now," she said. "I'll let myself out."

Not waiting for an answer, she pushed past him and all but ran to the garage where she retrieved her purse, threaded half a dozen plastic, cone-shaped collars over one arm and returned to the living room. Ken had picked up the box of bandages. "I'll carry these for you," he said.

At the truck, he slid the box onto the passenger seat. She dropped the collars onto the floorboard and slammed the door, then hurried around to the driver's side. "You look ridiculous in this big old wreck," he said, coming around to the driver's side as she hoisted herself up into the seat.

"I've got more important things to worry about."
She turned the key and the engine roared to life.

"Be careful," he said. "And be careful of that cop.
I don't trust him."

"I do," she said, and slammed the door, maybe
a little harder than necessary. She drove away, but
when she looked in the rearview mirror, Ken was
still standing there, watching her. She didn't think
he was a killer, but she was glad she had decided not
to date him anymore. She had never been completely
comfortable with him. And while she trusted Ryder
to have her best interests at heart, she couldn't say
the same about Ken.

ON SATURDAY AFTERNOON the parking area around the
ranch house at the Walker Ranch was so packed with
vehicles that a person could have been forgiven for
thinking the wedding day had been moved up, Darcy
thought as she maneuvered the truck into a parking
spot. A steady stream of young people made their
way to the bonfire in front of the house where Darcy
found Emily Walker greeting everyone.

Ryder caught her eye from the other side of the
bonfire and joined her. "Are all these people in
the wedding party?" Darcy asked. She recognized
Tammy Patterson, who worked for the *Eagle Mountain Examiner*, and Fiona Winslow, who waited tables at Kate's Kitchen. Dwight and Gage from the
sheriff's department were there, and Dwight's new
wife, Brenda Stinson. A few other people looked familiar, though she couldn't name them.

"Some of them. Others are people from town, and some visitors." He indicated a dark-haired man in a sheepskin jacket and cowboy hat. "That's Cody Rankin, a US Marshal who's one of the groomsmen. To his left is Nate Hall. He's a fish and wildlife officer—another groomsman."

"We ought to be safe here with all these law enforcement officers," she said.

"When you're in the profession, you end up hanging out with others in the profession a lot," Ryder said. "But there are plenty of civilians here, too." He nodded toward a pair of men in puffy parkas, knit caps pulled down low over their ears. "Those two are students Emily knows from Colorado State University. They came to Eagle Mountain on their winter break to ice climb and got trapped by the snow."

As she was scanning the crowd, Ken arrived. He saw her standing with Ryder and frowned, but didn't approach. Darcy was glad. After their uncomfortable encounter last night, she intended to avoid him as much as possible.

Emily climbed up on a section of tree trunk near the fire and clapped her hands. She wore a white puffy coat, and a bright pink hat, skinny jeans tucked into tall, fur-topped boots. Her long, dark hair whipped in the wind and her face was flushed from excitement or the fire, or both. "All right, everybody. I think everyone's here," she said. "I think you all know each other, but I wanted to introduce Jamie Douglas. She's been in town for a while, but she's the newest deputy with the Rayford County Sheriff's Department."

A rosy-cheeked brunette, who wore her hair in twin braids, waved to them.

"And last, but not least, we have Alex Woodruff and Tim Dawson." Emily indicated the two men Ryder had pointed out. "They live in Fort Collins and go to school at CSU."

Everyone waved or said hello to Alex and Tim, who returned the greetings. "All right," Emily said. "Let's get this party started." She pulled a handful of cards from her coat pocket. "I want everyone to form teams of two to three people each. Here are the lists of items you need to find. The first team to find all the items on the list wins a prize. Gage, please show everyone the prize."

Gage stepped forward and held up a liquor bottle. "What if you don't like Irish cream?" someone in the crowd asked over the oohs and ahhs of other guests.

"Then you give it to me, because it's my favorite," Emily said. She held up her phone. "It's two o'clock now. Everybody meet back here at four and we'll see who has the most items. We have plenty of food and drinks to enjoy around the bonfire, too. Now, come get your lists."

Ryder took Darcy's arm. "Let's team up together," he said.

"All right."

He went forward and got one of the cards, then rejoined her and they leaned in close to read it together. "A bird's nest, animal tracks, red berries, spruce cones, old horseshoe, mistletoe," Ryder read. "How are we supposed to collect animal tracks?"

"We can take a picture," Darcy said. "Where are we going to find a rock shaped like a heart with all this snow?"

"Maybe down by the creek." He handed her the list. "Did you bring snowshoes?"

They retrieved their snowshoes and put them on, then set out in the wake of other partygoers, everyone laughing and chattering. For once it wasn't snowing. Instead, the pristine drifts around them sparkled in the sun, the dark evergreens of the forest standing out against an intensely turquoise sky. "Emily must live a charmed life to get weather like this for her party," Darcy said as she tramped across the snow alongside Ryder.

"I'm hoping this break in the weather lasts," Ryder said. "The highway department is blasting the avalanche chutes today, and they've got heavy equipment in to clear the roads. With luck they can get everything open again by Monday morning."

"Will that help you with your case?" she asked. "Having the roads open?"

He glanced at her. "It will. But I don't want to talk about that today." He pointed a ski pole toward an opening in the woods. "Let's head to the creek, see if we can find that rock. And maybe the bird's nest, too."

"Are birds more likely to nest along creeks?" she asked.

"I have no idea. You're the animal expert here."

She laughed. "I can tell you about dogs and cats, some livestock, and a little about ferrets and guinea pigs. I don't know much about wild birds except they're pretty."

"Did you always want to be a veterinarian?" he asked.

"I wanted to be a ballerina, but short, awkward girls don't have much a chance at that," she said. "Then I wanted to be a chef, an astronaut or the person who ran the roller coaster at Elitch Gardens. That was just in third grade. I didn't settle on vet school until I was a sophomore in college, after I got a part-time job working at an animal hospital. I thought I would hate it, but I loved it."

"It's good to find work you love."

"What about you?" she asked. "Do you love your job?"

He glanced down at her, his expression serious. "I do. I like doing different things every day and solving problems and helping people."

"Is it something you've always wanted to do?" she asked.

"I went to college to study engineering, but attended a job fair my freshman year where the Colorado State Patrol had a booth. I'd never even thought about a law enforcement career before, but after I talked to them, I couldn't let go of the idea. I talked to some officers, did a couple of ride-alongs—and the rest is history." He stopped and bent to peer into the underbrush. "There's red berries on that list, right?"

"Yes."

He leaned forward and reached into the brush, and came out with a half dozen bright red berries clustered on a stem. "That's one down," he said. He handed the berries to her. "Stash those in my pack."

She had to stand on tiptoe—not an easy feat in snowshoes—in order to unzip the pack and put the berries inside. He crouched a little to make it easier. "Ready to keep going?" he asked.

She nodded and fell into step behind him this time as the woods closed in and the path narrowed. "How did you meet the sheriff?" she asked.

"We met in the state police academy," he said. "We just really hit it off. We kept in touch, even after he signed on with the sheriff's department in Eagle Mountain and I went to work for CSP. I visited him here on a vacation trip and fell in love with the place. When a job opening came up, I jumped on it." He looked over his shoulder at her. "How did you end up in Eagle Mountain?"

"Kelly visited here and came back and told me it was the perfect place to open a practice," she said. "There were a lot of people moving in, a lot of area ranches, and only one solo vet, so she thought we'd have plenty of business. I was ready to get out of the city so I thought, why not give it a try?"

"Will you stay, now that she's gone?"

She stopped. "Why wouldn't I stay?" Leaving hadn't crossed her mind.

He turned back toward her. "I hope you will stay," he said. "I just didn't know if it was something you'd want to do—or be able to afford to do."

She nodded. "Yeah, the money thing might be a problem. But I'm going to try to find a way to make it work. This is home now."

"An awfully tiny home," he said.

She laughed. "It's cozy and it's cheap," she said. "Maybe it wouldn't be practical for a family, but it's perfect for me right now."

The clamor of shouts ahead of them distracted her. Something crashed through the underbrush toward them, and Tim Dawson emerged onto the trail just ahead of them. "It's mine!" he shouted, waving what at first appeared to be a ball of sticks over his head. As he neared them, Darcy realized it was a bird's nest. Laughing and whooping, he ran past her, followed by his friend, Alex Woodruff.

She and Ryder started forward again, only to have to move off the trail again to allow Ken and Fiona to pass. "That jerk stole our bird's nest," Fiona said as she passed them.

"It was a jerk move, but there are probably other nests," Ryder said.

Fiona stopped, panting. "That's what I told Ken, but he's too furious to listen to reason." She bent forward, catching her breath. "Fortunately, those two are too fast, so I don't think he'll catch them."

"Do you want to hunt with us, instead?" Darcy asked. Not that she wasn't enjoying spending this time alone with Ryder, but she knew enough about Ken in a bad temper that she didn't want Fiona's afternoon ruined.

"Good idea to switch teams," Fiona said. She straightened. "It's sweet of you to offer, but I saw Tammy and Jamie up the creek a ways. I think I'll join them." She waved and headed back the way she had come.

Ryder and Darcy set out again and in another few minutes they reached the creek. The area near the trail was deserted, but tracks in the snow veered to the left along the bank. Ryder turned right. A few minutes later he stopped, putting an arm out to stop Darcy. "Animal tracks," he said, pointing to a row of tiny paw prints in the snow.

While he pulled out his camera and took several photographs, Darcy crouched to examine the tracks more closely. "I think they might be a weasel or something."

"I thought you didn't know about wild animals," he said.

"No. But they look a lot like a ferret. And ferrets are related to weasels."

Ryder pocketed his phone. "We have berries and animal tracks. What else is on the list?"

"The bird's nest and the rock shaped like a heart. A horseshoe—I don't think we're going to find that here."

"We can save the horseshoe for last. I know where the Walkers put all their old ones."

"Then we also need a spruce cone and mistletoe."

He scanned the trees around them, then took a few

steps forward and plucked an oval brown cone from a tree. "One spruce cone," he said and handed it over.

She closed her hand around the cone and turned toward his backpack, but froze as her gaze landed on a familiar clump of leaves in the tree over their heads. "Isn't that mistletoe?" she asked.

Ryder looked up, and a grin spread across his face. "It is."

"How are we going to get it down?" It had to be ten feet up the tree.

He looked down again, into her eyes, and her heart fluttered as if she'd swallowed butterflies as she realized they were standing very close—so close she could see the rise and fall of his chest as he breathed, and make out the individual lashes framing his blue eyes. He put a hand on her shoulder and she leaned in, arching toward him, and then he was kissing her—a slow, savoring caress of his lips, which were warm and firm, and awakening nerve endings she hadn't even known she had.

She moaned softly and darted her tongue out to taste him, and the gentle pressure of the kiss increased until she was dizzy with sensation, intoxicated by a single kiss. She opened her eyes and found he was watching her, and his mouth curved into a smile against his. She pulled back a little, laughing. "That's some really powerful mistletoe," she said.

"I'm thinking we have to get some to keep now." He looked up at the green clump of leaves, which grew at the end of a spindly branch of fir.

"You can't climb up there," Darcy said. "The tree

would never support your weight. And there aren't any branches down low to hold on to."

"Maybe I can throw something and knock some down."

"Throw what?"

"I don't know. A big rock?"

She looked toward the creek. Though snow obscured the banks and ice glinted along the edges, the water in the center of the channel was still flowing, and lined with rocks. "I'm not going to stick my hand in that freezing water," she said.

He stripped off his gloves and handed them to her. "I will."

"A picture is probably good enough," she said as he kicked out of his snowshoes.

"I told you, I like to solve problems." He took a step forward and immediately sank to his knees in the soft snow.

She put a hand over her mouth, trying to suppress a giggle. "Ryder, I really don't think—"

A scream cut off her words—an anguished keening that shredded the afternoon's peace and tore away the warmth Darcy had wrapped herself in after Ryder's kiss. "Who is that?" she asked.

Ryder fought his way out of the drift and shoved his boots back into the snowshoes. "It came from downstream," he said and headed out, leaving Darcy to keep up as best she could.

Chapter Nine

The screams had died down by the time Ryder reached the crowd of people on the stream bank. Gage turned at Ryder's approach, his expression grim. Next to him, his sister Emily stood with her face in her hands, drawing in ragged breaths, clearly trying not to cry. Tammy and Jamie both knelt in the snow, Tammy sobbing loudly.

"What's going on?" Ryder asked Gage. But then he saw the woman half-submerged in the shallow creek, hands and feet bound with silver duct tape, blood from the gash at her throat staining the water pink.

Behind him, Darcy made a choking noise. He turned to look at her, but Emily had already put her arm around her and was leading her away. "Travis is on his way," Gage said. "And Dwight. And probably Cody and Nate, too."

Ryder made himself look at the body in the water again. Fiona's knit cap had come off and her shoulder-length brown hair was spread out around her head, moving in the current of the stream as if blown by a gentle wind. "This must have just happened," he said, keeping his voice low. "Darcy and I saw her maybe half an hour ago. She and Ken Rutledge were chasing those two college guys—Tim and Alex— down the trail. She said Tim had stolen a bird's nest they had found. Ken was going after them. She decided to turn around and try to find Tammy and Jamie." He nodded to the two women kneeling in the snow. Emily and Darcy were beside them now, urging them up and away from the creek.

Tammy's sobs had quieted, and Jamie helped her to stand, then joined Gage and Ryder on the bank. "We didn't touch anything," she said. "I looked and I didn't see anyone else around here, or any obvious tracks."

Thrashing sounds in the brush heralded the arrival of Travis. "I sent Dwight to round up the rest of the guests and get them to the house," Travis said. He scowled at the scene beside the creek. "We need to get everybody out of here," he said.

"I'll take the others up to the ranch house," Emily said. Pale, but composed, she took Darcy's hand. "Darcy will help me."

The lawmen stood beside a large cottonwood, the bare branches forming a skeletal canopy over their heads while Emily and Darcy persuaded Tammy to come with them. When the others were out of sight up the trail back to the house, they began to work.

Gage and Jamie cordoned off the scene while Ryder took photographs. All the blood had washed away by now, leaving Fiona looking more like a mannequin than a human, her skin impossibly pale. Or maybe it only helped to think of her that way. She looked cold, sprawled in the icy water, though he knew she couldn't feel the chill anymore. She would never feel anything again, and the fact that she had been killed minutes after he saw her, when he was located less than a quarter mile away, gnawed at him.

Travis returned from a walk down the creek bank and the lawmen gathered under the tree once more. "The snow is churned up on this side of the creek for a good five hundred yards," he said. "There are some indistinct snowshoe tracks—probably from the guests on the scavenger hunt. No tracks on the opposite bank that I could find. My guess is the murderer walked in the water when he had to, and on trampled ground the rest of the time."

"So we're looking for a person or persons with blood on his clothes and wet feet," Gage said.

"He might not have any blood on him," Jamie said. "If he had her in the creek, facing away from him, he could reach in front of her, cut her throat and all the spray would go out in front and into the water."

"You say she was with Ken when you and Darcy met her on the trail?" Travis asked Ryder.

"He passed us first," Ryder said. "Well, Tim and Alex ran past us, and a few seconds later Ken ran past. Fiona was a few seconds behind him. She stopped to talk to us for a few more seconds, then turned and went back the way she came. She said she was going to catch up with Tammy and Jamie and hunt with them."

"She never found us," Jamie said. "We didn't hear or see anything of her until we came across her body."

Ryder was silent, recreating the scene in his head. "When Darcy and I got to the creek, where the trail stops at the creek bank, all the other tracks had turned left," he said. "We turned right and didn't see any other tracks."

"Could she have turned off the trail before she reached the creek?" Travis asked.

"I don't think so," Ryder said. "The brush is pretty thick on either side of the trail in there. She was wearing snowshoes, like us, so it would have been tough to maneuver through the underbrush."

"Emily and I were searching along the creek and we saw Jamie and Tammy ahead of us," Gage said. "We stopped to talk to them, and then started all searching together. We didn't see Fiona until we stumbled over her body."

"Did you see anyone else?" Travis asked.

Gage shook his head. "No."

"I told Dwight not to let anyone leave until we've questioned them," Travis said. "I want to know where everyone was and what they were doing when she was killed."

"The murderer isn't necessarily one of your guests," Ryder said. "It wouldn't have been that hard to find out this party was going on up here this afternoon. The killer might have taken it as a personal challenge to kill under a bunch of cops' noses, so to speak."

"Or maybe it's a copycat," Jamie said. "Someone with a grudge decides to get rid of Fiona and make it look like a serial killing."

"We'll look into Fiona's background," Travis said. "But I never heard anything about her having trouble with anyone."

"Why doesn't anyone around here get killed in a nice warm building?" Medical Examiner Butch Collins trudged into view, his booming voice the only clue to his identity, the rest of him concealed by a calf-length leather duster, a yards-long red wool scarf wrapped several times around his throat, the ends trailing down his back, a black Stetson shoved low over his ears, oversize dark glasses shading his eyes. He stopped in front of them and whipped off the glasses. "And while I'm ordering up the perfect murder, it needs to happen on a weekday, when coming to see you people is a good excuse for getting out of the office, instead of away from a nice warm fire in my own home."

"When we catch the killer, we'll be sure to pass along your request," Gage said.

Butch surveyed the body in the creek. "I hope you catch him soon," he said. "I'm tired of looking at lovely young women whose lives have been cut short." He shrugged out of his backpack and set it in the snow. "I'll be done here as soon as I can, so we can all get warm."

"Ryder, I want you and Gage to go up to the house

and start questioning people," Travis said. He didn't say *before one of them tries to leave* but Ryder knew that was what he meant.

The two men didn't say anything on their trek to the ranch house. Ryder's mind was too full of this new development. How had the killer been so close, and he hadn't had any inkling? Was one of the people waiting for him at the ranch house responsible for this and the other murders?

Emily must have been watching for them. She met them at the front door. "Everyone is in the living room," she said. "I had Rainey make hot chocolate for everyone—with whiskey or schnapps if they wanted—and plenty of snacks."

Conversation rose from behind them. "They don't sound too upset," Gage said.

"They were, at first," Emily said. "Then I had everyone show their scavenger hunt finds and got them to talking. It's not that everyone isn't horrified, but I didn't see any point in dwelling on the tragedy— and I didn't think you'd want them talking about it amongst themselves. Not before you'd had a chance to question them."

"Good thinking." Gage patted her shoulder. "Is everyone here?"

"Everyone," she confirmed.

A woman appeared in the doorway behind Emily. Nearly six feet tall, her blond hair pulled back in a tight ponytail, blue eyes lasering in on them from a weathered face. "These are for you," she said, pushing two mugs of hot chocolate toward them. "Get those coats and boots off and warm up by the fire before you go to work."

"Ryder, this is our cook, Rainey Whittington," Gage said. "In case you haven't noticed, she's bossy."

"Hmmph." She turned and left the room.

Ryder sipped the chocolate—it was rich and creamy. His stomach growled—he'd have to snag some of the hors d'ouevres he'd spotted on trays around the room to go with the chocolate.

He and Gage left their boots and coats in the foyer and moved into the next room—a large space with windows on two sides, a massive stone fireplace, soaring ceilings and oversize cushioned sofas and chairs. Almost every seat was filled with men and women, who looked up when Gage and Ryder entered.

Some of the women looked as if they had been crying. Most of the men showed tension around their eyes. "What's going on out there?" Ken Rutledge demanded.

"The medical examiner is at the scene," Gage said. He sipped his chocolate, watching the others over the rim of his cup. The two college guys, Alex and Tim, fidgeted. Tammy looked as if she was going to cry again. Ken prodded the fire with the poker.

Darcy cradled a mug with both hands and met Ryder's gaze. She looked calm, or maybe a better word was resigned.

"We're going to need to question each of you," Gage said. "To find out where you were and what you were doing shortly before Fiona's body was found."

"You don't think one of us killed her, do you?" Alex asked.

"You might have seen or heard something that could lead us to the killer," Gage said.

Rainey appeared in the doorway with a fresh tray of hors d'ouevres, a thin, freckled young man behind her with a second tray. She began passing the food. The young man walked up to Ryder with his tray. "I'm Rainey's son, Doug," he said.

Ryder took a couple of the sausage balls from the tray. "Thanks."

Gage shook his head and Doug moved on. "Ken, why don't you come in the library with me and Ryder," he said.

Ken jumped up and followed them down a short hallway to a small room just past the area where everyone had gathered. "You think because I was teamed up with Fiona that I had something to do with her death," he said. "But I don't know what happened to her. She didn't even tell me she wanted to split up—she just left."

"Why don't you sit down?" Gage motioned to an armchair. He and Ryder arranged the desk chair and another armchair to face him. Ken looked flushed and agitated, his face pale. His jeans, Ryder noted, were wet from the knees down.

"When I saw you on the trail, you were chasing Alex and Tim," Ryder said. "What was that about?"

"They stole the bird's nest Fiona and I found by the creek," Ken said. "I wasn't going to let them get away with that, so I chased them."

"Did you catch them?" Gage asked.

Ken looked sullen. "No. They must have veered off the trail into the woods."

"How far did you chase them?" Gage asked.

"I don't know. Not that far, I guess. It's too hard to run in snowshoes."

"What did you do after you stopped chasing them?" Ryder asked.

"I went looking for Fiona. I figured she'd be waiting for me, back on the trail, but she'd disappeared."

"Did that upset you?" Gage asked. "When you couldn't find her?"

"I was a little annoyed, sure. But I didn't kill her."

"You were annoyed because she ditched you," Ryder said.

"I thought maybe she got lost or something. Most women aren't good with directions."

Gage and Ryder both stared at him. "What?" Ken asked. "It's true."

"Okay, so you were by yourself, for how long?" Gage asked.

"I don't know. Twenty minutes? I was trying to find the others."

The desk chair squeaked as Gage shifted his weight. "Did you find them?" he asked.

"No," Ken said. "I finally gave up and came back here. That's when I heard what happened to Fiona. I feel sick about it."

"How did your pants get so wet?" Ryder asked.

Ken flushed. "I fell in the creek getting the bird's nest out of the tree. That's when those jerks came along and got it, while I was in the water. Fiona was screaming at them to stop and they just laughed."

"How did you and Fiona come to team up?" Ryder asked.

"I asked her to come with me. She wasn't here with anybody, so I figured, why not?"

"Had the two of you ever dated?" Ryder asked.

"Nah. We'd flirted some, when I had dinner at Kate's Kitchen. I was thinking about asking her out. I figured this would be a good way to get to know each other better."

"While you were looking for Fiona, did you see anyone else?" Gage asked. "Talk to anyone?"

He shook his head. "No. Not until I got back to the house. Travis was here, and his fiancée. Maybe some other people." He shrugged. "I just wanted to get inside and get warm. Then they told me about Fiona and I couldn't believe it. I mean, I thought this guy killed women in their cars. What's he doing out in the woods?"

Good question, Ryder thought. They sent Ken on his way. "What do you think?" Gage asked when he and Ryder were alone again.

"I don't know," Ryder said. "Maybe he's telling the truth. Or maybe he caught up with Fiona and slit her throat."

"But first he bound her wrists and ankles with duct tape and no one else saw or heard a thing?" Gage grimaced. "I'm thinking it had to be a job for two people."

"Let's talk to Tim and Alex," Ryder said.

Tim Dawson and Alex Woodruff had the easy-going, slightly cocky attitudes of young men for whom everything in life came easy. They dressed casually, in jeans and fleece pullovers and hiking boots, but the clothes were from expensive designers. They had straight teeth and stylish haircuts, and Alex wore a heavy copper and gold bracelet that wouldn't have looked out of place in an art gallery. He and Tim shook hands with Ryder and Gage, and met their gazes with steady looks of their own. "You've certainly got your hands full, investigating something like this," Alex said. "I don't imagine a sheriff's department in a place like Eagle Mountain is used to dealing with serial murderers."

"You might be surprised," Gage said, which had the two younger men exchanging questioning looks.

"How did you two end up in Eagle Mountain?" Gage asked when they were all seated in the library.

"We heard the ice climbing here was good," Tim said.

"Tim heard the ice climbing was good and wanted to come," Alex said. "I sort of invited myself along."

"Why is that?" Gage asked.

Alex shrugged. "I didn't have anything better to do. Getting away for a few days sounded like a good idea."

"We didn't plan on getting stuck here," Tim said.

"But we're making the best of it," Alex said.

"What are you studying at the university?" Ryder asked.

"Business," Tim said.

"Psychology." Alex's smile flashed on and off so quickly Ryder might have imagined it. "So this whole case interests me—as an observer."

"How did you come to be invited here today?" Gage asked.

"We know Emily from school," Alex said.

"Alex knows her," Tim said. "He introduced me when we ran into her in town a few days ago and she invited us to come." He shrugged. "It was fun until that girl was killed."

"Did you know the woman who died?" Gage asked.

They both shook their heads.

"Take us through the afternoon," Gage said. "What you did and when."

The two exchanged glances. Alex spoke first. "We got the list and decided to head to the creek. I guess a lot of people did that, but we ran to get ahead of them."

"Why the creek?" Ryder asked.

"It seemed to me that a lot of the items on the list could be found there," Alex said. "And I was right. We found the heart-shaped rock and the red berries right away. And then we got the bird's nest."

Tim made a noise that was almost like a snicker.

"Where did you find the bird's nest?" Ryder asked.

"That big blond guy—Ken—was standing on the creek bank in the snow, trying to get to this nest up high. He had hold of a branch and was trying to bend the tree down toward him."

"Except he slipped and fell into the water," Alex

said. "When he let go of the branch, the tree sprang back upright, and the nest flew out of it and landed practically at Tim's feet."

"So I picked it up and ran," Tim said. "The guy was screaming bloody murder, and so was the woman, too, but hey, I figure 'finders keepers.'"

"Losers weepers," Alex added.

"What happened next?" Ryder asked.

"You know," Tim said. "You saw. We took off, with the blond coming after us. He couldn't run that fast in snowshoes, and he gave up pretty quick."

"What did you do next?" Gage asked.

"We kept on finding the stuff on the list," Tim said. "We had everything but the horseshoe when the cops herded everyone back to the house."

"We figure we must have more items than any-one else," Alex said. "We're bound to win the prize."

"Did you see Fiona or Ken again after you ran off with the bird's nest?" Ryder asked.

"No," Alex said. "We didn't see anyone until that cop told us to go back to the house." He stretched his arms over his head. "Are you going to keep us here much longer?"

"Do you have somewhere else you need to be?" Gage asked.

"Not really." Alex grinned. "But it's Saturday night. We thought we'd go out, have a few beers, maybe meet some women."

"Where are you staying?" Gage asked.

"My aunt has a little cabin on the edge of town,"

Tim said. "It's a summer place, really, but it's okay. At least we're not paying rent."

Gage took down the address and both men's cell phone numbers. "That's all the questions I have." He looked at Ryder.

"That's all I have for now," Ryder said.

Tim and Alex stood. "You know where to find us if you need more," Alex said.

They ambled out of the room, shutting the door softly behind them. Gage let out a sigh. "Both of them working together could have done it," he said.

"They could have," Ryder said. "Or they could just be a couple of cocky college guys who didn't do anything but swipe a bird's nest that really didn't belong to anyone, anyway. They're not wet from being in the creek and they don't have blood on them."

"They might have a change of clothes in their vehicle or their pack," Gage said. "And Jamie was right about the blood—if they were careful, they wouldn't get much, if any, on them."

"We'll check their backgrounds, maybe talk to the aunt and their neighbors at that cabin," Ryder said.

A knock on the library door interrupted him. "Come in," Gage called.

Travis stepped inside and closed the door behind him. "How's it going?" he asked.

"Not much to go on yet," Gage said. "We've talked to Ken and Tim and Alex. That's all the non-law enforcement men. Except for Doug, the cook's son. I guess we'd better talk to him."

"I sent Jamie back early and she and Dwight interviewed the women," Travis said. "None of them saw or heard anything."

"Anything turn up at your end?" Ryder asked.

"We'll go over the body more closely tomorrow, but we found this." He took an evidence envelope from the inside pocket of his jacket and passed it over. Ryder stared at the single square of water-soaked pasteboard. A business card, the words Ice Cold barely legible on the front.

"It's the same killer," Ryder said. "Not a copycat. The same man or men who killed Kelly and Christy."

"It's the same one," Travis said. "He's challenging us right under our noses now."

Chapter Ten

Darcy arrived home to a chorus of complaining cats and the beginnings of more snow. She dealt with the cats by serving up fresh seafood delight all around, and dispensed with the snow by turning her back on it, drawing the shades and standing under the strong stream of a hot shower until the icy chill that had settled over her hours ago had receded and the tension in her shoulders and neck began to relax.

She and Ryder had exchanged a brief goodbye as she filed out of the ranch house with the rest of the non-law-enforcement guests. Earlier she had given her version of their encounter on the trail with Ken and Fiona to the female deputy, Jamie. "I'll call you when I can," Ryder said, and squeezed her hand.

She checked the locks on her doors and windows again, turned on the outside lights and settled on the sofa with a fresh cup of tea and a peanut butter sandwich—her idea of comfort food. She had just picked up a favorite Regency romance novel and turned to the first chapter when strains of Vivaldi sounded from her cell phone.

Spirits lifting, she snatched up the phone, but her mood dropped again when she saw that the call wasn't from Ryder as she had hoped, but from Kelly's mother. "Darcy, I hope I haven't caught you at a bad time." Cassidy Farrow spoke with a tremor as if she was very old, though she was probably only in her early fifties.

"Not at all." Darcy tucked her feet up beside her and pulled a knitted blanket up to her knees. "What can I do for you?"

"I don't know, really. I just…I just wondered if you've heard anything about…about Kelly's case. If they're any closer to finding out who did this awful thing." Her voice caught, and Darcy pictured her struggling to regain her composure.

"I know the officers are working very hard to find out who killed Kelly," Darcy said. Should she mention the other women who had died? No. That would only be more upsetting, surely.

"I hate to keep calling the Colorado State Patrol," Mrs. Farrow said. "They're always very nice, of course. And they tell me they'll contact me when they know something, but then I don't hear anything, and we can't even get there to see our girl, or to take her…her body for the funeral. It's just so awful."

"It is," Darcy said. "It's the most awful thing I can imagine." She grieved terribly for her friend—how much worse the pain must be for Kelly's mother.

"It doesn't even seem real to me." Mrs. Farrow's voice was stronger now. "I don't think it will be until

I see her. I keep dreaming that there's been some mistake, and that she's still alive."

"I catch myself thinking that, too," Darcy said. "I wish she were still here. I miss her all the time."

"The officer I spoke to said they were sure the woman they found was Kelly."

"Yes," Darcy said, speaking softly, as gently as she could. "It really was Kelly."

The sobs on the other end of the line brought tears to her own eyes. As if sensing her distress, Elinor crawled into her lap, and the other cats arranged themselves around her, a furry first-aid team, offering comfort and protection.

"I'm sorry," Mrs. Farrow said. "I didn't mean to call and cry like this. I just wanted to talk to someone who knew her, who understood how wonderful she was."

"Call anytime," Darcy said. "It helps to talk about her. It helps me, too."

"Thank you. I'll say goodbye now, but we'll be in touch."

"Goodbye."

She ended the call and laid the phone back on the table beside her. She turned back to her book but had read only the first page when headlights swept across the windows, and the crunch of tires on her gravel drive made her clamp her hand around the phone again. She glanced toward the loft where the gun lay in the drawer of the table beside her bed. Then she shook her head and punched 911 on her phone. She wouldn't hit the send button yet, but she'd be ready.

The car stopped and the door creaked open. Darcy wanted to look out the window, but she didn't want to let whoever was out there know her location in the house. Footsteps—heavy ones—crossed to the house and mounted the steps to her little front porch, then heavy pounding shook the building. "Darcy, it's me, Ken. Please let me in. I need to talk to someone."

Her shoulders sagged, and annoyance edged out some of her fear. "Ken, I really don't want to have company right now," she said.

"Just let me in for a few minutes," he said. "Today has been so awful—for us both. I just need to talk."

She wanted to tell him no—that she just wasn't up to seeing him right now. But he sounded so pitiful. Fiona had been his partner in the scavenger hunt—to have her killed must have been a shock to him. Sighing, she unlocked the door and let him in. "You can only stay a few minutes," she said. "I really am exhausted."

He had changed clothes since leaving the ranch and wore baggy gray sweatpants and a University of Wisconsin sweatshirt. His hair was wet as if he had just gotten out of the shower. "Thanks," he said. "I was going crazy, sitting at the house with no one to talk to."

"Do you want me to make you some tea?" Darcy asked.

"No. That's okay." He began to pace—four steps in one direction, four in another. "I can't believe this is happening," he said.

"I can't believe it, either." Darcy settled on the

sofa and hugged a pillow to her chest. Three women dead—it was hard to accept.

"That cop as good as accused me of murdering that woman."

Of course. Ken wasn't upset because Fiona had died. He was agitated because he had been questioned. "He's just doing his job," she said. "The cops questioned everyone."

Ken stopped and faced her. "Why are you defending him? Is there something going on between you two?"

"No!" But her cheeks warmed at the memory of the kiss they had shared under the mistletoe. Maybe *something* was happening with her and Ryder—but she wasn't clear what that something might be. Or what it might turn into.

Ken began to pace again, running his fingers through his hair over and over, so that it stood straight up on his head, like a rooster's comb. "You shouldn't be here by yourself," he said. "You should come and stay at my place. No one will bother you with me around."

"No one is going to bother me here."

"You can't know that."

She wasn't going to waste her breath arguing with him. She picked up her now-cold tea and sipped, waiting for him to calm down so she could ask him to leave.

More headlights filled her window. "Who's that?" Ken demanded.

"I don't know." She stood and went to the door. A

few moments later a light knock sounded. "Darcy? It's me, Ryder."

Relief filled her and she pulled open the door. She wanted to throw her arms around him, but thought better of it, feeling Ken's stare burning into her back. "What are you doing here?" Ken asked, his tone belligerent.

"I wanted to make sure Darcy was all right after the upsetting events of this afternoon," Ryder said. He moved into the room and shut the door, but kept close to Darcy. "Why are you here?"

"Darcy and I are friends. I wanted to make sure she was all right, too."

"Thank you for checking on me, Ken," Darcy said, hoping to defuse the situation by being gracious. "I'll be fine. You can go now."

"Is he staying?" Ken asked.

"That really isn't your concern," she said. She patted his arm. "Go home. Try to get some rest."

He hesitated as if he intended to argue, then appeared to think better of it and moved past Ryder and out the door. As he pulled out of the drive, Ryder gathered Darcy close. "Your heart is pounding," he said into her hair. "Did he frighten you?"

"No. Just annoyed me." She looked up at him. "I think he has a habit of rubbing people the wrong way."

"What did he want?"

"He was upset. He seemed to think you believe he killed those women."

"We haven't identified anyone as our main suspect."

"Ken is annoying, but I can't believe he's a killer," she said. "And you said his alibis checked out."

"Alibis can be faked," he said. "And right now it's my job to be suspicious of pretty much everyone."

She started to protest again that Ken couldn't be the murderer—but how much of that was a true belief in his innocence, and how much was her desperate desire not to be wrong again about a man she had trusted? She probably would have defended the man who raped her, too—until he turned on her. Was she making the same mistake with Ken?

She put her hand on his shoulder, the leather of his jacket cold beneath her palm. "You're freezing," she said. "And you must be exhausted."

"I'm all right," he said.

"At least let me fix you some tea or soup."

"I wish I could stay, but I need to get over to the sheriff's department. I just wanted to make sure you were okay."

"You're going back to work?" she asked. "Does this mean you have a suspect?"

He shook his head. "I couldn't tell you if I did, but no. No suspects yet. We need to look at the evidence we gathered today and see if we find something we've missed before."

"You don't really think one of the party guests is the killer?" she asked. Everyone had seemed so nice—people she either already thought of as friends, or whom she looked forward to getting to know better.

"We just don't know." He kissed her cheek. "All you can do is be extra careful."

He started to pull away, but she wrapped her arms around his neck and tugged his lips down to hers. She hadn't intended to kiss him so fiercely, had only wanted to prolong the contact between them, but as soon as their lips met the last bit of reserve in her burned away in the resulting heat. She lost herself in the pleasure of that kiss, in the taste of him, in the power of his body pressed to hers, and in her own body's response.

He seemed to feel the same, his arms tightening around her, fitting her more securely against him, his lips pressed more firmly to hers, his tongue caressing. She felt warmed through, safer and happier than she had felt in a long time. They broke apart at last, both breathing hard, eyes glazed. He stroked his finger down her cheek. "I wish I didn't have to go," he said.

"I wish you didn't have to go, either."

He stepped back, and she reluctantly let him. "Lock the door behind me," he said.

"I will."

"If Ken comes back here, don't let him in," he said.

"All right," she said.

She didn't want to let anyone in—into her home, or her life, or her heart. That had been her policy for years. But Ryder had breached those barriers and the knowledge both frightened and thrilled her. He wasn't a killer. Ryder would never hurt her. She knew that, but that didn't mean he didn't have the power to hurt her. Maybe not physically, but if you gave your heart to someone, you risked having it broken. She had been so wrong about a man before—would she ever really be able to trust her judgment again?

RYDER WAS THE last to arrive in the situation room at the sheriff's department. He filled a mug from the coffeepot at the back of the room, then settled at the table next to Gage. Like Ryder, most of the others still wore the clothes they had had on that afternoon. Only the sheriff and Dwight were in uniform—Ryder assumed because they were on duty.

"Let's get started," Travis said from the front of the room. "I've asked Cody and Nate to sit in, since they were at the ranch this afternoon."

US Marshal Cody Rankin and Department of Wildlife officer Nate Hall nodded to the others.

Travis moved to the whiteboard. "Let's start by summarizing the information we learned this afternoon," he said. "Jamie, you helped interview the women. Anything there?"

"Ryder and Darcy appear to be the only people who saw Fiona after she and Ken set out on the scavenger hunt," Jamie said. "No one thought it was odd for her to be with him. Several said they were laughing together when they split up from the rest of the group to start the hunt. No one saw any strangers or anything they thought was odd or out of place."

Travis nodded. "About what we got from the men, too."

"I don't think any of the women had the physical strength to overcome Fiona," Jamie said. "Even two women working together would have had a hard time, and she would have fought and screamed. Someone would have heard."

"There were no signs of struggle in the stream or on the bank," Dwight said.

"There were a lot of footprints in the soft snow," Ryder said. "Too many to tell who they belonged to."

Travis picked up a sheet of paper from a stack on the end of the conference table. "The medical examiner says Fiona was struck on the back of the head," he said. "It wasn't enough to kill her, but it probably would have knocked her out, at least long enough to restrain her."

"So whoever killed her comes up behind her, hits her in the head with a big rock before she can say anything," Gage said. "She falls, he wraps her up in duct tape, slits her throat and leaves."

"That's different from the way he handled Kelly and Christy," Ryder said.

"Probably because he was in a hurry," Gage said. "He was out in the open, with lots of people around. He needed to get her down quickly."

"So we're pretty sure it's a man," Travis said. "I think it's safe to rule out the law enforcement personnel who were at the party."

"That leaves Ken, Alex and Tim," Ryder said.

Travis wrote the names on the whiteboard. "Ken was the last person seen with Fiona," he said. "He's big and strong enough to take her down without too much trouble, and he was alone with her. Alex and

Tim could have worked together. They're new to the area, and we don't know much about them."

"Ken has strong alibis for the other two murders," Ryder said. "And we're assuming all three women were murdered by the same person because of the business card."

"Do we have any idea what the significance of Ice Cold might be?" Jamie asked.

"I've been working on that." Dwight, who had been rocked back in his chair, straightened. "On-line searches haven't turned up anything—no businesses by that name. Maybe the killer is bragging about how 'cool' he is."

"Or how fearless and unfeeling?" Jamie suggested. "Nothing can touch him because he's ice cold."

"We know this guy likes to show off," Ryder said. "Leaving the cards at the scene of each killing is a way of bragging. And killing Fiona when he was pretty much surrounded by cops is pretty arrogant."

"Tim and Alex struck me as arrogant," Gage said.

"Let's check their alibis for the other two killings," Travis said. He glanced at his note. "And there's one other man on the scene we need to check."

"Doug Whittington," Gage said.

"Right," Travis said.

"The cook's son," Ryder said, remembering.

"It would have been fairly easy for him to slip away from the house and follow Fiona and Ken into the woods," Travis said.

"What do you know about him?" Ryder asked. "Has he worked for your family long?"

"Rainey has been with us for at least ten years," Gage said. "Doug only showed up a couple of months ago."

"My parents agreed he could stay to help Rainey with the extra workload of so many wedding guests," Travis said. "She promised to keep him in line."

"What do you mean, *keep him in line*?" Ryder asked.

"He has a record," Travis said. "In fact, he just finished a fifteen-month sentence in Buena Vista for assault and battery."

"He beat up his girlfriend," Gage said. "Broke her jaw and her arm."

Jamie made a face. "So a history of violence against women. That definitely moves him up my list."

"Let's check him out," Ryder said. "But be careful. Make it seem routine. Not like we suspect him."

"We'll keep a close eye on all our possible suspects," Travis said. "Whoever did this may think he can kill right under our noses, but he'll find out he's wrong." He laid aside the marker he'd been using to make notes on the whiteboard. "Dwight, I want you and Ryder to interview Doug tomorrow. Since his mother is so closely associated with our family, Gage and I should keep our distance for now."

"I want to talk to Alex and Tim tomorrow, too," Ryder said. "Double-check their alibis for the other murders."

"If the roads open up tomorrow, we'll have someone rush the forensic evidence we've collected to the lab," Travis said.

"I wouldn't hold your breath on that," Gage said. "The snow is really coming down out there."

"We'll do what we can," Travis said. "For now the rest of you go home and think about what we know so far. Maybe you'll come up with an angle we haven't examined yet."

Ryder said good-night to the others and climbed into his Tahoe. But instead of driving to the guest house he rented on the edge of town, he turned toward the address for the cabin Alex and Tim said belonged to their aunt. He wouldn't stop there tonight; he just wanted to check it out and see what those two might be up to. And if they weren't home, he might take a little closer look at the place.

He had just turned onto the snow-covered forest service road that led to the cabin when he spotted a dark gray SUV pulled over on the side of the road. The vehicle was empty, as far as he could tell, but there were no houses or driveways nearby. Had someone broken down and left the car here? An Eagle Mountain Warriors bumper sticker peeked out from the slush that spattered the vehicle's bumper. Where had he seen this vehicle before?

He parked his Tahoe in front of the SUV and debated calling in the plate, which was almost obscured by slush. He climbed out of his vehicle and walked back toward the SUV to get a better look. He had just pulled out his flashlight when shouting to his right made him freeze. A cry for help, followed by cursing and what might have been jeers. He played the light over the side of the road and spotted an opening in the brush. It appeared to be a trail. As the shouting continued, he sprinted down the narrow path into the woods.

Chapter Eleven

The trail ended in a clearing at the base of ice-covered cliffs. Ryder shut off his light and stopped, watching and listening. Moonlight illuminated two young men in Eagle Mountain High School letter jackets standing at the base of a frozen waterfall, while a third young man dangled precariously from the ice. "Help!" the man stranded on the ice called.

"Chicken!" one of his companions jeered.

"You don't get credit unless you make it all the way up," the third man said.

"This ice is rotten," the first man said. "This was a stupid idea."

"You took the dare," the second man said. "That's the rules. To get credit, you have to complete it."

Ryder switched on the light, the powerful beam freezing the three teens. They stared at Ryder, expressions ranging from defiance to fear. Ryder moved toward them. "I heard the shouting," he said. "What's going on?"

"Just doing some climbing." The first young man—blond, with acne scars on his cheeks—spoke.

He slouched, hands in pockets, not meeting Ryder's eyes.

Ryder played the beam of light over the young man on the ice. He balanced on a narrow ledge on one foot, hands dug into the ice in front of his chest. "You okay up there?" he called.

"I'm fine." The man spoke through clenched teeth.

"Odd time of night to be climbing," Ryder said. "And shouldn't you have ropes and a helmet?"

"He said he's fine." The second young man spoke. "Why don't you leave us alone?"

"He doesn't look fine." Ryder pulled out his phone. "I'm going to call for help."

"No!" The man on the ice sounded frantic. "I'll be okay. I just need to find the next footho—" But the word ended in a scream as the ledge holding him broke and he slid down the ice.

Ryder sprinted forward, though the young man's companions remained frozen in place. He was able to break the kid's fall, staggering back under the sudden weight, then dropping hard to his knees on the snowy ground, the young man collapsed against him. They stayed that way for a long moment, catching their breath.

The sound of an engine roaring to life made Ryder jerk his head around. The climber's companions were gone. "Looks like your friends ditched you," he said.

The young man grunted and tried to stand, but his left leg buckled when he tried to put weight on it.

Ryder knelt beside him. "You're hurt," he said. "Lie still. I'll call for help."

"I don't need help." The young man tried to stand and succeeded this time, though he favored his left leg. "It's just a sprain." He glared at Ryder. "I would have been fine if you hadn't interfered."

"I'd better take you home," Ryder said.

Sullen, the young man limped ahead of him down the trail. Ryder waited until he was buckled into the passenger seat of the Tahoe before he spoke. "What's your name?" he asked.

"Greg Eicklebaum," he said. "You can drop me off at the school. I'll walk home from there."

"You can't walk home with a bad ankle." Ryder started the Tahoe. "What's your address?"

Greg reluctantly rattled off an address in one of Eagle Mountain's more exclusive neighborhoods. "My parents are going to freak when a cop shows up at the door," he said.

"What did your friends back there mean about the climb not counting if you didn't finish?" Ryder asked.

"It was nothing. Just stupid talk."

"I gathered you made the climb on a dare."

Greg said nothing.

"What other dares have the three of you tried?" Ryder asked.

Greg stared out the window. "I don't know what you're talking about."

"Did you decide to break into some houses on a dare? Maybe the tiny house out at Lusk Ranch where the veterinarian lives? Or the Starling place on Pine Drive? Fred Starling said he thought the guy he surprised was wearing a letter jacket like the one you've got on."

Greg slumped down farther in his seat. "I don't have to talk to you," he said. "I'm a minor and you can't question me without my parents around."

"You're right. Let's wait and talk to your parents. I'm sure they'll be interested in hearing about this dare business."

Greg sat up straighter. "We're not doing anything wrong," he said. "It's just, you know, a way to pass the time. So we dare each other to do stuff, like climbing without ropes. Stupid, maybe, but it's not against the law."

"Attempting to break in to someone's home is against the law."

"I don't know anything about that."

"What other kinds of dares have you done?" Ryder asked.

"Gus ate a live cricket." Greg grinned. "It was disgusting."

"So there's you and Gus. Who's the third kid?"

Greg's expression grew closed off again. "I don't have to say."

"That's okay. I'll run the plate on his vehicle and find out."

Greg glared at him, then slumped down in his seat.

"The night of those break-ins, a woman was murdered," Ryder said.

"Are you trying to pin that one on us, too?" Greg asked.

"The murder wasn't far from the Starling house. The weather was bad and there weren't many people out. The person or persons who attempted the break-in might have seen the murderer, or his car."

"Can't help you."

"Think about it," Ryder said. "The sheriff might be willing to overlook an attempted burglary charge in exchange for evidence that helps us track down a killer."

"Right."

When Ryder pulled into the driveway at the Eicklebaum house, no lights showed in the windows. Greg unsnapped his seat belt and was opening the door before Ryder came to a complete stop. "Looks like nobody's home," he said. "Thanks for the ride." Then he was out of the Tahoe and sprinting up the drive.

Ryder waited until the young man was in the house, the door shut behind him. He could have waited for the parents to return, or he could come back later to talk to them, but he doubted they would be able to shed any light on the situation. He'd run the plates on the SUV, and let Travis and his men know about the three young men and their series of dares. He couldn't prove they were the ones behind the break-in at Darcy's house, but it felt right. And if he could find the right pressure to put on them, they might have some evidence that could help break this case.

"GOOD MORNING, Trooper Stewart."

Ryder was startled to be greeted by Adelaide

Kinkaid when he entered the sheriff's office Sunday morning. "What are you doing working on a Sunday?" he asked.

"No rest for the wicked," she said.

"She doesn't think we can manage without her," Gage said as he joined Ryder in the lobby.

"You can't," she said. "And as long as there's a killer terrorizing my town, I don't see any sense sitting at home twiddling my thumbs. It's not as if at my age I'm going to take up knitting or something."

"I have a job for you," Ryder said. He handed her a piece of paper on which he'd written the license plate information from the SUV Greg's friends had driven. "Find out who this vehicle is registered to."

Adelaide studied him over the top of her lavender bifocals. "Does this have something to do with the killer?"

"Probably not. But I still need to know."

"All right. But next time call it in to the highway patrol."

"Yes, ma'am." Ryder grinned, then followed Gage into his office where Dwight was already slouched in the visitor's chair.

Dwight straightened and stifled a yawn. "I guess you're here to go with me to interview Doug Whittington," he said.

"That's the plan." Ryder leaned against the doorjamb. "No rush. I'd like to get the information on that license plate from Adelaide first."

"What's up with the plate?" Gage asked.

Ryder told them about his encounter the night before with Greg Eicklebaum. "The plate belongs to the SUV they were in. His friends drove off without him, so I didn't get their names, though I take it one of them has the first name of Gus."

"Gus Elcott." Adelaide spoke from the doorway. "The SUV is registered to his father, Dallas, but Gus is the one who drives it."

"What do you know about Gus?" Ryder asked her. Adelaide was known for having her finger on the pulse of the town.

"He's the star forward on the high school basketball team. An only child of well-off parents, which means he's spoiled, but aren't they all these days?" Her eyes behind the bifocals narrowed. "Why? What's he done?"

"Nothing that I know of," Ryder said. "I caught him and some friends ice climbing in the dark without safety equipment. One of them fell and sprained his ankle and I took him home."

"Oh. Well, I suppose if that's the worst trouble they get into, we should be thankful." She left them.

Gage moved over to the door and shut it. "Now, tell us what's really going on," he said.

"I'm not sure," Ryder said. "Greg said something about a series of dares they were doing, and apparently there's some kind of point system. I take it whoever racks up the most points wins. Wins what, I don't know, and Greg wouldn't elaborate. But I think Greg and Gus and one other kid, whose name I don't know yet, were behind the attempted break-ins at Darcy's house and at Fred Starling's the night Christy O'Brien was killed."

"Fred said he thought the burglar wore a high school letter jacket," Gage said.

"Yeah," Ryder said. "And Darcy said the car that pulled out of her driveway that night was a dark SUV. And I saw three high school boys at the grocery store not long before the break-ins."

"It doesn't sound like we have enough evidence to charge them with anything," Dwight said.

"No," Ryder agreed. "But there's a chance those boys saw something that night that could help us track down the murderer—a vehicle, or maybe the murderer himself. We just have to find a way to make them talk."

"Maybe we gather more evidence about the burglaries and use that to put pressure on them," Gage said. "Offer to make a deal."

"It's worth a try," Ryder said. "Right now we don't have much else."

Dwight stood. "Maybe after today we'll have more," he said. "You ready to go interview Doug?"

"Be warned that Rainey isn't going to welcome you with open arms," Gage said. "She's very protective of her son."

"Any particular reason why?" Ryder asked.

"Apparently, his dad was out of the picture early on, and she raised him by herself. It really broke her heart when he went to jail. She's determined to keep him from going back." He pulled a folder from a stack on the corner of his desk. "Take a look at this before you go out there. Dwight's already seen it."

Ryder read through the file. Doug Whittington had been convicted two years previously of beating up his girlfriend during a drunken argument. He broke her jaw and her arm and cracked several ribs. She had ended up in the hospital, and he had ended up in jail. After he had served fifteen months of a two-year sentence, he was eligible for parole. He looked up at Gage. "Did he come to the ranch right after he was paroled?"

Gage nodded. "Rainey begged my parents to let him stay with her on the ranch until he could get on his feet again. He had completed both anger management and alcohol rehab while behind bars, and wasn't going to mess up in a household with two lawmen as part of the family."

"If he is the killer, he's taking a big risk, murdering women while two lawmen are in and out of the house practically every day," Dwight said.

"This particular killer seems to enjoy taking risks and taunting lawmen," Ryder said. "So he would fit that pattern."

Gage took the folder Ryder handed him. "I hope he has nothing to do with this. It's going to be messy for my folks if he does, but we have to check it out. Still, Rainey isn't going to be happy."

Twenty minutes later Ryder parked in front of the ranch house and he and Dwight made their way up a recently shoveled walkway. Emily answered their knock, dressed in ripped jeans and a button-down shirt, her hair piled in a loose knot on her head and her feet bare. "Mom and Dad are away, but Travis told me you were coming," she said, ushering them inside. "He asked me not to say anything to Doug. He and Rainey are both in the kitchen."

She showed them into the kitchen, a modern, light-filled space with expanses of cherry cabinets and black granite countertops. The cook, Rainey, was rolling dough on the kitchen island while Doug chopped carrots by the sink. Rainey looked up as they entered, her gaze sweeping over them. "Hello, officers," she said, her tone wary.

"You remember Sergeant Stewart and Deputy Prentice from my party yesterday, don't you?" Emily asked.

"We need to ask Doug a few questions," Ryder said.

At the sink, Doug stopped chopping and raised his head, but he didn't turn around.

"Doug can't tell you anything," Rainey said.

"You don't know what we need to ask him," Ryder said.

"It doesn't matter." Rainey went back to rolling dough. "He doesn't socialize with folks in town. He stays here at the ranch with me and keeps his nose clean. He's had culinary training, you know. He plans to open his own restaurant one day, or maybe do catering. He's been a big help to me, preparing for this wedding."

"If he hasn't done anything wrong, then he doesn't have anything to worry about," Dwight said.

Rainey sniffed. "Go ahead and ask, then. He doesn't have anything to hide, do you, Doug?"

Doug wiped his hands on a dish towel and turned to face them. He had a square, freckled face under closely cropped hair, his nose off-kilter as if it had been broken and not set properly. "What do you want to know?" he asked.

"I'll leave you all to it," Emily said and slipped out the door.

Ryder turned to Rainey. "If you could excuse us a moment," he said. "This won't take long."

"It's my kitchen and I'm not leaving." She assaulted the dough on the counter with vigorous strokes from her rolling pin. "And he's my son. Anything you want to ask him, you can ask in front of me."

Ryder and Dwight exchanged looks. They could always insist on taking Doug down to the sheriff's department to interview, but that would no doubt cause trouble for the sheriff and his family. And it might be interesting to see how Rainey reacted to their questions. There was still the possibility that the killer had had an accomplice. "All right," he said and took out his notebook. "During the party yesterday, what were you doing?"

"I worked with Mom, in the kitchen here," he said. "We made snacks for the party."

"Did you take a break from the work anytime?" Ryder asked. "Maybe step outside for a cigarette?"

Doug looked at his mother, who had given up all pretense of rolling out dough and stood with her arms crossed, watching them. "Mom doesn't like me to smoke," he said.

"But did you smoke?" Ryder pressed. "Maybe stepped outside to grab a quick cigarette?"

Doug nodded slowly.

"When?" Ryder asked.

"I dunno. A couple of times. But I didn't go far." He nodded toward the back door. "Just behind the woodpile out there."

Ryder walked to the door and looked out the glass at the top. A wall of neatly stacked wood extended from the corner of the house, forming a little alcove between the back door and the side of the house. "Did you see anyone while you were out there?" he asked. "One of the party guests, or maybe someone who wasn't supposed to be there? Did you speak to anyone?"

"No. I try to stay back, so no one sees me."

"How long were you out there?" Dwight asked.

"A few minutes. Maybe ten. As long as it takes to smoke a cigarette."

"What about last Tuesday?" Ryder asked. "What were you doing that day?"

He looked again to his mother, his gaze questioning. "I dunno," he said. "I guess I was here."

"That's the day they found those women," Rainey said. "And yes, he was here. With me. What are you implying?"

Ryder ignored the question. "You were here all day?"

"Are you calling me a liar?" Rainey moved around

the counter toward him. She was almost as tall as Ryder, and though she had left the rolling pin on the counter, he was aware that it was still within reach, as were half a dozen knives in a block on the edge of the counter.

"If you can't remain quiet, Mrs. Whittington," Ryder said, "I'll have to ask you to leave."

She said nothing, but didn't advance any farther toward him.

Trusting Dwight to keep an eye on her, Ryder turned his attention to Doug. "Did you know Kelly Farrow or Christy O'Brien or Fiona Winslow?" he asked.

"No," Doug said.

"You'd never seen any of them around town, or spoken to them?" Ryder asked.

"I saw Fiona at the restaurant where she worked," he said. "She waited on my table once."

"Did you speak to her?" Ryder asked.

"I maybe said hello." He shifted his weight and shoved his hands in the pockets of his jeans. "There's no law against that."

"She was a very pretty woman," Ryder said.

"They were all pretty," Doug said.

An innocent statement, maybe, but it gave Ryder a chill. "I thought you said you didn't know Kelly or Christy."

"I saw their pictures in the paper."

"Did you ask Fiona to go out with you?" Ryder asked.

"What makes you think that?" Doug asked.

"Just a guess. Maybe you asked her out and she turned you down. When you saw her at the party, it reminded you of that and made you angry. Maybe you followed her into the woods and confronted her."

"No!" Doug and Rainey spoke at the same time.

"How dare you make up lies like that about my son," Rainey said. "Just because he made a mistake once, people like you want him to keep paying for the rest of his life. Instead of going out and finding the real killer, you can just pin these murders on him and your job is done."

"I haven't accused your son of anything," Ryder said.

"Does the sheriff know you're here?" she asked. "I can't imagine he'd put up with you bullying someone who is practically a member of his own family."

"Can Mr. or Mrs. Walker, or someone else, confirm that you didn't leave the ranch on Tuesday?" Ryder asked Doug.

"I don't know," he said. "I guess you'd have to ask them."

"Please don't ask them." Rainey's tone had turned from strident to pleading. "You'll only embarrass all of us. Doug was here because he was with me. I make it a point to keep him busy. He doesn't need to go to town for anything."

"He obviously went to town at some point and met Fiona at the restaurant," Dwight said.

"He was with me that day," Rainey said. "I keep him with me."

Dwight returned his notebook to his pocket.

"That's all for now," he said. "I may have more questions later."

They left the kitchen. The living room was empty, so they let themselves out of the house. Ryder stopped on the way back to the Tahoe and looked around. Four cars were parked in front of the house, with another couple of trucks over by the horse barn. "A lot of vehicles," he said.

"The Walkers and Emily live here, along with Rainey and Doug, a ranch foreman and a couple of cowboys," Dwight said. "Cody Rankin is staying here until the wedding, and there are probably people in and out all day—delivery people, the veterinarian and farrier, other service people."

"So it would be easy for Doug to have slipped away while his mother was busy," Ryder said.

"Maybe," Dwight said. "But what's his motive?"

"He thought the women who were killed were pretty. If they turned down his advances, he might have taken it personally."

"He served time for assaulting a woman," Dwight said. "Not a stranger, but a woman he knew. And the crime was more violent and spontaneous. These crimes feel more planned out to me."

Ryder nodded. "His mother is worried about something," he said and resumed the walk to his vehicle. "Something to do with Doug."

"I got that feeling, too," Dwight said. "He might not be guilty of murdering Fiona and the others, but she thinks he's guilty of something."

"Or maybe she's lying about Doug having been

with her every day, all day," Ryder said. "Her guilt over the lie is what I'm picking up on."

"She said she keeps him on the ranch with her, and pretty much doesn't let him out of her sight," Ryder said. "But it might be possible he could slip out without her knowing."

"Anything is possible," Dwight said. "We could get a warrant to search his room. Maybe we'd get lucky and find a stack of Ice Cold calling cards."

"I don't think we have enough evidence to get a warrant," Ryder said. "Right now he has an alibi we can't disprove for all the killings. We don't have a motive, and the crime he was convicted of isn't similar enough to these murders to justify a search—at least not from a judge's point of view."

"I wonder if he has access to a computer and printer?" Dwight asked.

"I'll bet there's one somewhere in that house." Ryder glanced over at the big ranch house. "But without a warrant, we can't legally find out what's on it."

"We don't have much of anything, really," Dwight said. "That's the problem with this case—lots of guys who might be a killer, but no proof that any of them are."

"Yeah." Ryder's hands tightened on the steering wheel. "It feels like we're in a race, hurrying to catch this guy before he strikes again." A race that, right now at least, they were losing.

Chapter Twelve

By Monday Darcy was feeling much calmer. Fiona's murder had been very upsetting, but Darcy had managed to bring her feelings under control and focus on her work. "You've got a new patient in room two," Darcy's receptionist, Stacy, said when Darcy emerged from the kennels that afternoon where she'd been checking on a corgi who had had a bad tooth removed that morning. Churchill the corgi, more familiarly known as Pudge, was sleeping peacefully in a kennel, cuddled up on his favorite blanket, supplied by his indulgent owner.

"Oh?" Darcy accepted the brand-new patient chart, labeled Alvin. The information sheet inside listed a three-month-old Labrador puppy, Spike.

"The pup is adorable," Stacy said. "I should prepare you for the owner, though."

Darcy checked the sheet again. The puppy's owner was listed as Jerry Alvin. "What about him?" Had he given Stacy trouble already?

"He seems very nice," Stacy said. "But he's recovering from some kind of accident—his face is all bandaged and one arm is in a sling. I thought I should prepare you since it's a little shocking when you first see him."

"Oh, okay. Thanks." She closed the folder, then opened the door to exam room two.

Jerry Alvin's appearance was indeed a little shocking. Most of his head—with the exception of his eyes, ears and chin, was wrapped in bandages, and his left arm was enclosed in a black sling. He wore a black knit hat pulled down to his ears, tufts of blond hair sticking out from beneath it. "Hello, Dr. Marsh," he said, rising to greet her, and offering his hand.

"Hello, Mr. Alvin." She turned to greet the dog. "And hello, Spike."

Spike, a dark brown ball of fur, seemed thrilled to see her, jumping up and wagging his whole body. Darcy rubbed behind his ears and addressed his owner once more. "What's brought you in to see me today?"

"I was in a car accident." Alvin indicated the bandages. "Got pretty banged up. Spike was thrown from the car. He acts okay, but I just wanted to make sure he isn't hurt."

"When did this accident happen?" Darcy asked.

"Yesterday. I hit an icy spot on the highway and ran off the road, hit a tree. My head went through the windshield. I guess I'm lucky to be alive."

Darcy knelt and began examining Spike. The pup calmed and let her run her hands over him. "You say he's acting fine," she said. "No limping or crying out?"

"No. He landed in a snowbank, so I guess that cushioned his fall."

Spike certainly looked healthy and unharmed. Darcy picked him up and put him on the exam table. "He has a little umbilical hernia," she said. "That's not uncommon with some puppies. Chances are he'll outgrow it, but we should keep an eye on him."

"I'll do that. Thanks."

The hernia made her think of another puppy she had seen recently, with an almost identical umbilical hernia. Gage Walker's lab puppy was a twin to this dog—same age and size. He even had the same cloverleaf-shaped white spot on his chest. A chill swept over Darcy as she continued to examine the dog. If this wasn't the same puppy Gage had brought to her, then it was an identical twin. She glanced at Alvin. "Is something wrong?" he asked, leaning toward her.

"Nothing." She picked up the puppy and cradled it to her chest. "I'm going to check something in the back right quick. It won't take a minute." Before he could stop her, she exited the room and hurried to the back. She found her microchip reader in the drawer of the lab table and switched it on. With shaking hands, she ran it over the pup's shoulder. A number appeared on the screen. Darcy made note of the number, then carried the puppy to an empty kennel and slid it inside. The pup whined at her. "You'll only be in here a minute," she said and shut the door and slid the catch in place.

Then she hurried to the front office. "What's going on?" Stacy asked. "Did something happen back there?"

"What do you mean?" Darcy pulled Gage Walker's folder from the filing cabinet and spread it open on the desk.

"Mr. Alvin just ran out of here—without his dog."

Darcy looked up. "What?"

"He couldn't get out of here fast enough," Stacy said.

Darcy went to the window and peered out at the parking lot. Only her and Stacy's cars were visible. "Did you see what he was driving?" she asked.

"No." Stacy folded her arms. "Are you going to tell me what's going on or not?"

"Just a second." Darcy returned to the folder and compared the code the microchip scanner had displayed with the code registered to the microchip she had implanted in Gage's puppy, Admiral. They matched.

Stacy peered over her shoulder. "What are you doing with Gage's folder?"

"The puppy back there—the one Jerry Alvin called Spike—is Gage Walker's new dog."

"You mean that guy stole it?" Stacy's eyes widened. "So all those bandages must have been a disguise. But why bring it here?"

"I don't know." Darcy picked up the phone and punched in Gage's cell number. He answered on the third ring.

"Darcy," he said. "What can I do for you?"

"Gage, I have your puppy, Admiral, here at the office," she said.

"What? What happened? Where's Maya?"

"A man who said his name was Jerry Alvin brought him in to see me," Darcy said. "He was calling the dog Spike. As soon as I went into the back to check the dog's microchip, he ran out the front door."

"I'll be right over," Gage said.

Darcy went to the back and retrieved the puppy from the kennel. She wasn't comfortable letting it out of her sight until its real owner arrived. Ten minutes later Gage walked into the office, along with Maya and Casey. The little girl squealed and ran to envelop the puppy in a hug.

"We got in from school just a few minutes ago," Maya said. "We were frantic when we couldn't find Admiral. Gage called while we were looking for him."

"He's perfectly fine," Darcy reassured them. "Whoever took him didn't hurt him."

Gage took a small notebook from the pocket of his uniform shirt. "Tell me about this Alvin," he said. "What did he look like?"

"That's the thing," Darcy said. "I can't really tell you." She explained about the bandages and sling.

"It looked like a Halloween costume," Stacy said. "He said he'd been in a car wreck."

"He told me he ran off the road and hit a tree," Darcy said. "Even when he said that, I was thinking it didn't sound right. He said his face went through the windshield, but wouldn't the airbag have protected him from that? And even if he wasn't wearing a seat belt, it seemed he would have been hurt worse. And do they really bandage people up like that—like mummies?"

"How tall was he?" Gage asked. "What kind of build?"

Darcy and Stacy exchanged glances. "Just—average," Darcy said.

"Maybe five-ten," Stacy said. "Not too big, not too little."

"Hair color?" Gage asked. "Eye color?"

"He had a knit cap pulled over his hair, but there were some blond strands sticking out," Darcy said. "And I was so distracted by the bandages, I didn't notice his eyes."

"How was he dressed?" Gage asked.

"Jeans, a dark blue or black parka and the hat," Darcy said. "I didn't notice his shoes."

"The bandages and sling really drew all your attention, you know," Stacy said. "I guess that was the idea."

"Did you get a look at his car?" Gage asked.

Both women shook their heads.

Gage pocketed the notebook. "I'll ask the neighbors if they saw anyone around the house this afternoon."

"I'm so glad you thought to check the microchip," Maya said. She held the puppy now, stroking the soft brown fur. "I don't know what we'd have done if we lost him."

The front door opened and Ryder entered. "Darcy, are you all right?" he asked.

"I'm fine," she said. "Why wouldn't I be?"

"I stopped by the sheriff's department and Adelaide told me a guy showed up at your office who had stolen Gage's dog."

"He did, but he ran away when I took the dog into the back room to check the microchip," she said.

"I don't understand," Stacy said. "Why bring the dog here in the first place? It wasn't sick or hurt, and he had to have realized that in a town this small, the odds were good we had already seen the puppy." She tapped her chin. "You know, the more I think about it, the more I think this guy was trying to seem older than he was. Like—I don't know—a kid playing dress-up."

"You think this was a kid?" Darcy stared at her.

Stacy scrunched up her nose. "Not a little kid, but maybe a teenager?"

"I have an idea," Ryder said. "Maya, do you have a high school yearbook at your house?"

"Sure," Maya said. "I have a copy of last year's."

"Could you bring it to us? Now?"

"Oh. Okay." She took Casey's hand. "Come on, honey. Let's take Admiral home and get a book Trooper Stewart wants to look at."

"Why do you want to look at the school yearbook?" Darcy asked.

"Just a hunch I have about who might have done this. You take care of your next patient and I'll call you when Maya gets back with the book."

Darcy vaccinated a dachshund, and Maya and Gage returned together with the Eagle Mountain High School yearbook. "You think those daredevil high school students were behind this?" Gage asked as he handed over the yearbook.

"I think it's a possibility." Ryder opened the book. "What year is Greg Eicklebaum?" he asked.

"He's a junior," Maya said.

Ryder flipped to the pages for the junior class and found Greg's picture and showed it to Stacy and Darcy. They both peered at it, then shook their heads. "I was paying attention to the dog, not its owner," Darcy said.

"That's not the guy," Stacy said. "The hair was a lot lighter, and I'm pretty sure at least some of it was real."

"Try Gus Elcott," Gage said.

Ryder found Gus's picture, but it got a no also. "Try Pi Calendri," Maya said.

"Who names their kid Pie?" Ryder asked as he turned pages.

"It's short for Giuseppe," Maya said. "Apparently, a lot of Italians settled in this area at the turn of the last century to work in the mines. The Calendris have been here for generations. The story I heard is that Giuseppe is Italian for Joe. Someone started calling him Joe Pi, then it got shortened to Pi." She shrugged. "He hangs out with Dallas and Greg."

Ryder studied the photograph of a mature-looking blond. He turned the page toward Stacy. "What about him?"

"Bingo." She nodded. "That's him."

Darcy leaned over to take a look. "I think it could be him," she said. "Something about the chin…"

Ryder closed the book. "Why would Pi Calendri steal our dog?" Maya asked. "He's not even in any of my classes."

"Why don't we go talk to him and find out," Gage said.

Chapter Thirteen

The Calendri home was in the same neighborhood as the Eicklebaums', though the house was larger, with more spectacular views. An attractive blonde answered the door, and her carefully groomed brows rose at the sight of two law enforcement officers on her doorstep. "Is something wrong?" she asked.

"Mrs. Calendri?" Ryder asked.

She nodded. "We'd like to speak to Pi," Ryder said. "Um, that is, Giuseppe."

"What is this about?"

"We have a few questions for him," Gage said. "We'd like you and your husband, if he's home, to be present while we talk to him, of course."

"My husband isn't here," she said. "Should I call our lawyer?"

"It's just a few questions," Ryder said. "May we come in?"

She stepped back and allowed them to pass, then shut the door behind them. "Excuse me," she said and hurried up the stairs to their left. A few moments later not-so-muffled tones of argument sounded overhead, though the words were too garbled for Ryder to make them out. A few seconds later mother and son descended the stairs.

"Hello, officers." A handsome young man, neatly dressed in jeans and a button-down shirt, stepped forward and offered his hand. "My mother said you wanted to speak to me. Is this about that fender bender in the school parking lot yesterday afternoon? I'm afraid I wasn't there. I had practice."

"Pi is rehearsing for the school's production of *Guys and Dolls*," Mrs. Calendri said. "He has the male lead."

"So you're in drama," Gage said. He and Ryder exchanged looks. A drama student would know how to change his appearance and assume a different identity.

"Yes, sir. You're Ms. Renfro's husband, aren't you?" Pi asked.

"Yes."

"Come into the living room and have a seat and tell us what this is all about." Mrs. Calendri led them into a room that looked straight out of a top-end designer's showroom—all leather and hammered copper and carved cedar. A fire crackled in a massive gas fireplace. A large white dog rose from a bed in front of the fire and padded over to greet them, tail slowly fanning back and forth.

"Beautiful dog," Ryder said, scratching the animal's ears.

"That's Ghost," Pi said. He sat on the end of the

sofa. Ryder and Gage took chairs facing him. The dog sat beside the young man, who idly patted its back.

"You like dogs, I see," Ryder said.

"Sure," Pi said. "Who doesn't?"

"What is this about?" Mrs. Calendri asked.

"I have a dog," Gage said. "A chocolate Lab puppy, Admiral."

"Labs are great dogs," Pi said. "Do you plan to train him to hunt?"

"I hope to." Gage scratched his chin. "Funny thing, though. Someone took Admiral out of my yard this afternoon."

"That's terrible." Pi looked suitably shocked, though Ryder thought he wasn't ready for his professional acting debut just yet. "Do you know who did it?"

"We have a very good idea," Ryder said. "And we think you do, too."

"Are you accusing Pi of taking your dog?" Mrs. Calendri poised on the edge of her seat as if prepared to leap up and do battle on behalf of her child.

"Funny thing about cops," Gage said. "We're very security conscious. And when you have a family, you can't be too careful. Lots of us install security cameras in our homes." Ryder noticed that Gage hadn't said that he personally had a security camera, though he wanted Pi to think so.

"Not to mention, the receptionist at the vet clinic where you tried to pass off Admiral as your own made you for a teenager right away," Ryder said.

Pi tried to hold his expression of surprise, but

Ryder's words broke his resolve. He slumped, head in his hands. "It was just supposed to be a joke," he said. "I would never have hurt your dog, I promise. I would have returned him to your house before you even knew he was gone."

"Giuseppe! What are you saying?" Mrs. Calendri glared at her son. "You stole this officer's dog? Why?"

"You did it on a dare, didn't you?" Ryder asked.

Pi nodded. "At first, the dare was just to snatch the dog. But there's nothing really difficult or dangerous about taking a dog out of someone's yard." He sent Gage an apologetic look. "We didn't know about the security camera. So then we decided it would be worth more points if I tried to pass the dog off as my own. So we thought I should take it to the vet. If I could have fooled her, I'd be way ahead of the other guys on points."

"How many points would breaking into someone's house be worth?" Ryder asked.

Pi flushed. "I don't know anything about that."

"Pi, what are you talking about?" Mrs. Calendri asked. "What other guys?"

"Greg Eicklebaum and Gus Elcott," Ryder said. "They've been egging each other on in a series of dares, to see who can get away with various stunts without getting caught." He turned back to Pi. "Who's ahead?"

"Right now Gus is," Pi said. "After he put the bear statue from the city park on the high school gym roof the week after Christmas. He was sure nobody could beat that. That's why I had to do something really outrageous to top him." He buried his head in his hands. "Am I in big trouble for taking your dog? I promise I wouldn't have hurt him."

"You could be," Gage said. "That depends on whether or not you're willing to help us in another matter."

"Of course he'll help you," Mrs. Calendri said.

Pi sighed. "What do you want?"

"The night Christy O'Brien was killed—Tuesday, the fifth," Gage said. "You and Greg and Gus were out that night, in the snowstorm."

"I saw you in the parking lot of the grocery store," Ryder said. "You stood out because almost no one else was out in that weather."

"So? There's no law against being out at night," Pi said.

"Who else did you see that night? You may have seen the murderer, or his car."

"We didn't see anybody," Pi said. "That's the point, you know? Not to see anyone and not to let them see you."

"Except the veterinarian, Darcy Marsh, came home and surprised you trying to break in to her house, and a little while later Fred Starling did the same," Ryder said.

"I don't know what you're talking about," Pi said.

"We don't care about that right now," Gage said. "We want to know if you saw anyone else out that night. Any other car on the road, especially near Fred Starling's place."

"We weren't near Fred Starling's place," Pi said. "I can't help you."

"How do you know where Fred Starling lives?" Ryder asked. "We didn't mention an address."

Pi scowled. "This town is like, three blocks wide. I grew up here. I know where everyone lives. Mr. Starling was my Cub Scout leader when I was in second grade."

"He said he doesn't know anything that can help you." Mrs. Calendri stood. "If you want to talk to him anymore, you'll have to wait and do it when his father and our lawyer are present."

Ryder and Gage rose also and followed Mrs. Calendri to the door. In the hallway Gage turned back to Pi. "If you think of anything that might be helpful, call anytime," he said. "Oh, and if anything else happens to my dog, I'll come looking for you, and I won't just ask questions."

"I would never hurt a dog," Pi said. "I promise you."

Gage nodded, and both officers left.

When they were in Ryder's Tahoe again, he leaned back against the driver's seat and let out a long breath. "Those boys were responsible for both those attempted break-ins," he said.

"We'll never prove it," Gage said. "But at least we know it wasn't the murderer targeting Darcy."

"The boys didn't pretend to be an old woman with a dog, and I don't think one of them ran her off the road," Ryder said. "All three of them were playing on the varsity basketball team that night. I saw the roster when I checked Ken Rutledge's alibi."

"Right," Gage said. "I'm still holding out hope they saw something that night that can help us. We'll try questioning all three of them, but we'll have to be careful—probably bring them in to the station with their parents and their attorneys. I'll talk to Travis and see what he thinks."

"Good idea." Ryder started the Tahoe. "Want me to drop you at the station or your house?"

"My vehicle is at my house. And I need to check in with Maya and Casey. Casey isn't going to want to let Admiral out of her sight for the next month."

"I'm glad your dog is okay," Ryder said.

"Me, too. I believe Pi when he said he wouldn't hurt him, but we need to stop these stunts before somebody does get hurt." He was silent a moment, then chuckled.

"What's so funny?" Ryder asked.

"I can't believe a high school kid got that bear statue up on the roof of the gym. The statue is made of bronze. It must weigh a ton. I took the call and the look on the principal's face was priceless. It was all I could do to keep a straight face."

"Maybe we can declare Gus the winner of the contest and put an end to the dares," Ryder said.

"Yeah," Gage agreed. "We've got better things to do than deal with high school delinquents." They had a murderer to stop, and Ryder hated that it didn't feel like they were any closer to him than they had ever been. It was only a matter of time before he struck

again, and every woman in town was vulnerable—
even, or especially, Darcy.

DARCY WASN'T SURPRISED to see Ryder waiting for her
as she ushered her last patient of the day back into
the lobby. She busied herself removing her lab coat
and smoothing her hair while the woman paid her
bill. As soon as the door shut behind the woman,
Stacy demanded, "Well? Did you find out who took
Gage's pup?"

"It was a high school kid," Ryder said.

"I knew it!" Stacy pumped her fist.

"What did he want with Gage's dog?" Darcy
asked.

"He did it on a dare." Ryder came around the
counter to join them in the little office space. "We
think he and his friends were behind the attempted
break-in at your house, and at another house, the
night Christy O'Brien was killed."

Darcy sagged against the counter. "That's a relief," she said. "I mean, to know it was just a bunch
of kids." And not the killer—though she couldn't
bring herself to say the words out loud.

"Yes and no," Ryder said. "The kids aren't dangerous, but this does show how vulnerable you are
to someone who could mean harm. Especially while
we've got a killer running loose, you should be wary
of new clients."

"I'm not going to turn away paying customers—
or hurt animals," Darcy said.

He opened his mouth to protest and she rushed to

cut him off. She wasn't going to debate her business practices. "I've already made a policy of not going on any more house calls for new patients," she said. "And I won't see anyone if I'm here alone."

"I'll start asking every new patient for a copy of their driver's license," Stacy said. "They do it at my doctor's office—I don't see why I can't do it here."

"That's not a bad idea," Darcy said. "We'll be careful, I promise."

Ryder studied her, clearly displeased, but not saying anything. Stacy slung her purse over her shoulder. "I think I'll head home now." She looked from Ryder to Darcy. "You two don't need me here."

When she was gone Darcy steeled herself to argue with Ryder. "I can't shut down my business or put my life on hold because of the killer," she said. "Of course I'll be careful, but teenagers playing pranks don't have anything to do with that. They're a nuisance, but they're not dangerous."

"They aren't the ones who ran you off the road when you went on that bogus call," Ryder said. "We still don't know who was responsible for that. They might try again."

Her stomach hurt, the old fear squeezing at her. But she couldn't let fear run her life. If Ryder had his way, he'd want her to shut down the practice and move into a spare cell at the sheriff's department. As pleasant as it was to know he was concerned for her, she couldn't live like that. "I'll be careful," she said, softening her voice. "It's all any of us can do."

He nodded. "That doesn't mean I won't worry."

"And I think your worrying is sweet." She reached for her coat and he took it and held it while she slipped her arms into the sleeves. It was a little gesture, but it touched her. She turned and put her hands on his chest. "It means a lot to me," she said. "Knowing you care. But it unsettles me a little, too. I'm not used to that."

He covered her hands with his own. "I hope you could get used to it."

"Maybe I can. But I need time. And I need space, too. Okay?"

He looked into her eyes. Searching for what? she wondered. He stepped back. "Okay," he said. "I'll walk you to your car, then I have to get back to work. I won't rest easy until we've found this guy."

"I think all of us can say that," she said. And she wouldn't deny that it was comforting to have him walk her to her car—to have him watching over her.

RYDER REMINDED HIMSELF that Darcy was a smart, careful woman who would be on her guard against anyone who might harm her. She was perfectly capable of looking out for herself, and he really ought to be concentrating on the case. He'd always made it a point to seek out easy, uncomplicated relationships—that worked out best for everyone involved. But there was nothing easy or uncomplicated about Darcy. Yet, the thought of distancing himself from her set up a physical ache in his chest.

He tried to push the thought aside as he headed back to the sheriff's department—his home away from home these days, since his regular office on the other side of Dixon Pass was off-limits due to the still-closed roads. Gage saluted him with a slice of pizza. "There's more in the break room, if you hurry," he said.

Ryder helped himself to the pizza. "I thought you'd be home with your dog," he said when he rejoined Gage in his office.

"I'm on duty this evening," Gage said. "And the dog is fine—being showered with treats by Maya and Casey, who have vowed not to let him out of their sight."

Ryder sank into the chair across from Gage's desk. "I don't even know why I'm here," he said. "Except I keep hoping for a break in the case."

"You can help sort through the calls we've had from the public." Gage picked up the top sheet from a stack of printouts on his desk. "'My neighbor has a lot of guns and looks at me funny whenever I go out to my car. Maybe he's your killer.'" He tossed that sheet aside and selected another. "'I overheard a man at the café the other morning tell his wife that Fiona Winslow probably got in trouble because she was such a big flirt. I didn't get a good look at him, but if you find him, maybe he knows something.'"

"Are they all like that?" Ryder asked.

"So far. But we have to look at them all. Someone might come up with something. Oh, and I almost forgot." He pulled another sheet of paper from a different stack. "This came into the office for you this morning."

Ryder set aside the half-eaten slice of pizza and took the paper—a printout from the Colorado Department of Corrections. "Who is Jay Leverett and why do you want to know if he's been released from prison or not?" Gage asked.

"It's a man Darcy dated in Fort Collins," Ryder said. "The relationship didn't end well."

"And you thought he might have tracked her down here?"

"It's always possible." He glanced up. "You saw what he served time for?"

Gage nodded. "Sexual assault. And he was released two months ago."

"And the DOC has no idea where he is now." Ryder tossed the paper back onto the desk. "Do you know of anyone in town who fits his description?"

"Not offhand," Gage said. "But we have a lot of strangers stranded here by the storms. He could be one of them."

"And he could be our killer," Ryder said. "Or not. But it's one more lead to follow."

Adelaide appeared in the doorway. "If you men are finished stuffing your faces, there's someone here who wants to speak with an officer," she said. "Actually, two someones. Tourists."

"I'll take this," Gage said.

Ryder and Dwight followed Gage and Adelaide to the lobby, where Tim and Alex stood, studying the photographs displayed on the walls. "Hey, long time no see," Alex said.

"Adelaide said you wanted to talk to an officer?" Gage asked.

"Yeah," Tim said. "We want to report a crime."

"What sort of crime?" Gage asked.

"Someone tried to kill us," Alex said. "You've got a lunatic running around in your little town."

Chapter Fourteen

"You say someone tried to kill you?" Ryder studied the two men before him. Tim looked visibly shaken, but Alex was red-faced with anger. "What happened?"

"Come take a look at this." Alex motioned them toward the door.

Ryder, Dwight and Gage followed Alex and Tim out into the small front parking lot. Alex led the way to a gray Toyota 4Runner. "Some maniac tried to run us off the road," Tim said. "Look what he did to my ride." He walked around the car and indicated the bashed-in driver's side front quarter-panel.

"Was it a traffic accident, or was it deliberate?" Gage asked.

"Oh, it was deliberate," Alex said. "He aimed right at us."

"Come inside and tell us what happened," Gage said. He led the way to an empty conference room. He sat on one side of the table, with Alex and Tim on the other. Dwight sat next to him, while Ryder stood by the door. This wasn't his case—the two men had come to the sheriff's department to report a crime. But his interest in the men as suspects in his case made it reasonable for him to be present for the interview, though he planned to keep quiet and let Gage take the lead.

Gage leaned over and switched on a digital recorder that sat in the middle of the table. "I'm going to make a record of this," he said. "We'll transcribe your statements later and have you sign them. All right?"

Both men nodded. "Okay," Gage said. "Tell us what happened—where were you, when and all the details you can remember."

"We were out near Tim's aunt's cabin," Alex said. "On County Road Five. We were headed into town for dinner when this guy in a dark pickup truck turned out of a side road and headed toward us. He was driving really fast."

"Yeah, like maybe eighty miles an hour," Tim said. "Crazy, because the road has a lot of snow on it—packed down and drivable, but not that fast."

"Tim laid on the horn and moved over as far as he could, but the guy just kept coming," Alex said.

"It was like he was playing chicken or something," Tim said. "He headed straight for us and at the last minute sideswiped us."

"If he was going that fast and hit you, why didn't he lose control and go crashing into the trees?" Dwight asked.

Tim glanced at Alex. "He was lucky, and a good driver," Alex said.

"It would have been better if you had remained at the scene and called us," Gage said. "We'll send someone out to take a look. We may be able to determine his speed by skid marks."

"Good luck with that," Alex said. "It's all snow out there."

"You can see where we went into the ditch," Tim said. "And there's, like, glass and stuff from my busted headlight."

"All right," Gage said. "We'll check. In the meantime, can you tell us where you were Tuesday?"

Tim laughed. "I can't even remember what I had for breakfast yesterday."

"That was the day after that first big snowstorm, right?" Alex said. "The day those two women were killed."

"Yes," Gage said. "What were you doing that day?"

"We were hanging out at Tim's aunt's place, moaning about being stuck here for who knows how long," Alex said.

"Did you go out to a restaurant or bar or maybe to the store to buy groceries?" Gage asked. "Did you see or talk to anyone else?"

"Nah. We stayed in and got drunk," Tim said.

"No offense, but the idea of being stuck here with nothing to do when we could be back in the city, hanging out with friends, really bummed us out," Alex said.

"I thought you came here to ice climb," Gage said.

"Sure. But you can't even do that when it's snowing so hard you can't see in front of your face," Alex said.

"Yeah," Tim agreed. "We've pretty much climbed all the good local routes, so doing them again would be kind of lame."

"How have you been occupying your time while you're stranded here?" Dwight asked.

"Watching a lot of TV, playing video games," Tim said.

"That's why it was so nice of Emily Walker to invite us to her party," Alex said. "It was a lot of fun until that poor woman was killed."

"Did you get a good look at the driver of the truck that hit you?" Gage asked. "Did you get a license plate number?"

"I'm pretty sure the vehicle didn't have a front license plate," Alex said. "And the windows were tinted. I had the impression of a big person—probably a man, with broad shoulders. He was wearing some kind of hat, like a ball cap."

Gage looked at Tim, who shrugged. "Like he said, the windows were tinted. And I was too terrified to notice much of anything. I really thought we were going to be killed."

"Were either of you hurt by the impact?" Gage asked.

"My neck is pretty sore." Alex rubbed the back of his neck. "I think I might have whiplash."

"I'm just generally banged up," Tim said. "No permanent damage, I don't think."

"Your airbag didn't deploy," Dwight said.

Again, the two friends exchanged a look. "No," Tim said. "I wondered about that. Maybe it's defective."

"We were both wearing seat belts," Alex said. "I'm sure that saved us from more serious harm."

"We'll get someone out to the site and check it out," Gage said. "We don't have a lot to go on, but we'll do what we can, though I think you realize we're a small department, and we have more pressing concerns at the moment."

"I wanted to ask you about that," Alex said. He smiled, a tight grimace that made Ryder think he didn't use the expression often. "I think I told you I'm studying psychology at the university. I have a special interest in serial killers. I'm actually thinking of pursuing a career as a profiler, helping law enforcement."

"I really can't talk about the case," Gage said.

"Oh, I get that," Alex said. "I wouldn't ask you to reveal anything confidential. But I read in the paper that the killer has been leaving cards with the bodies of his victims—cards that say Ice Cold. I wonder what you think the significance of that might be. Is he trying to send a particular message? And to whom? Does he kill women because he sees them as emotionally cold? Does he think this about all women or do his victims symbolize a particular woman?"

"I don't have any answers for you," Gage said. He stood. "If you could stop by the station again tomorrow, we'll have your statements ready for you to sign, and we may have some photographs from the scene for you to look at and verify. Thanks for stopping by."

He and Dwight escorted the two out to the truck and watched them leave. When they returned to the lobby, Ryder asked, "What do you make of that?"

"They're lying about something," Gage said.

Dwight nodded. "I got that, too," he said.

"The truck was damaged," Ryder said.

"It was," Gage said. "I'm just not sure the damage happened the way they said."

"What about those questions he asked?" Ryder asked. "About the killer?"

"Lots of people are fascinated by serial killers," Dwight said. "I imagine most psychology students find the topic interesting."

"How did the information about those cards get in the paper?" Ryder asked.

"Tammy Patterson was at the party at the ranch Saturday," Gage said. "She's a reporter for the paper. She probably heard about the cards there."

"I wish she hadn't publicized it," Ryder said.

"Nothing we can do about it now." Gage shoved his hands in his pockets. "Alex raised some interesting points," he said. "Ones we should look at."

"They don't have an alibi for the day Kelly and Christy were killed," Ryder said.

"No," Gage said. "But the weather was bad that day. Most people were probably staying at home, watching TV, playing video games and drinking. It doesn't prove they were guilty of anything."

"We aren't getting anywhere with this case," Ryder said.

"When we find out what those two are lying about, maybe we'll have something to work with," Gage said.

"I AM NOT going to let you eat lunch cooped up here in the office again." Stacy, purse in hand, handed Darcy her coat after she had sent her last patient of the morning on her way Tuesday.

"I don't mind staying in." Darcy slipped out of her lab coat and hung it on a peg by the door. "It's a good time to catch up on paperwork." Since Kelly's death, she had fallen into the habit of bringing food from home or from the grocery store deli, and eating at her desk.

"Lunch is supposed to be a break from work," Stacy said. "So you come back in the afternoon refreshed. Besides, if you go to lunch with me, neither one of us is alone. It just seems safer to me for women to travel in groups around here, at least until that Ice Cold Killer is caught."

"Ice Cold Killer?" The name gave her a jolt. "Where did you get that?"

"That's what the paper is calling him. Apparently, he leaves a business card with those words on it with each of the bodies of the women he's killed." She shuddered. "Creepy. I wouldn't stay anywhere by myself for ten seconds, much less a whole lunch hour."

"I'm sure I'm perfectly safe here," Darcy said,

though even as she uttered the words, a shiver of fear ran through her. "I keep the door locked."

"You keep thinking that way if it helps you sleep at night," Stacy said. "As for me, I'm scared half to death, and I'd appreciate the company."

Though Stacy's tone was joking, Darcy sensed some truth behind her words. She hadn't read the latest issue of the paper, but news of a serial killer snowed in with the rest of the town had everyone on edge. And she had noticed an uptick of men accompanying the women who brought their pets in to see her. Maybe she and Stacy keeping each other company wasn't such a bad idea. She collected her purse from the bottom drawer of the filing cabinet. "All right. I'll go to lunch with you."

They headed for Kate's Kitchen, always a favorite. But the black ribbons adorning the door reminded them that Fiona Winslow had worked here, which momentarily quieted their conversation. Stacy waited until they had placed their orders before she spoke. She stripped the paper off a straw and plopped it into her glass of diet soda. "It's just so weird that a serial killer would end up here, in little Eagle Mountain. What's the attraction?"

"I guess killers take vacations and go to visit relatives, like anyone else," Darcy said. "He got caught by the snow like a lot of other people."

"And while he's here he decides he should kill a few people?" She grimaced. "It's beyond creepy."

"I know the sheriff's department and every other law enforcement officer in the area is working really hard to track him down," Darcy said. "They're bound to catch him soon. There aren't that many people in this town, and he can't leave."

"Yeah. You have to hope the killer really is a stranger who got stuck here—and not someone we've all known for years. That would freak me out. I mean, how could someone hide that side of himself?"

"It happens all the time," Darcy said. The man who had raped her had seemed like another good-looking, charming fellow student—until he had refused to let her leave his apartment one night, and had turned what had started as a pleasant date into a nightmare.

"I guess it does," Stacy said. "I mean, the news reports always have some neighbor talking about 'He was such a nice, quiet man. He kept to himself and didn't hurt anybody.'"

The waitress—an older woman whose name tag identified her as Ella—delivered the soup and sandwiches they had both ordered. Darcy picked up her spoon.

"Speaking of law enforcement officers," Stacy said. "What's the story with you and Ryder?"

Darcy blinked. "Story?"

"He's not hanging around the office so much because of the case," Stacy said. "Or at least, that's not the only reason." She picked up half a sandwich. "And didn't the two of you team up at Emily Walker's party last Saturday? How was that?"

"It was fun." Darcy sipped her own drink. "Until it wasn't."

"Yeah, not the most romantic of circumstances," Stacy said. She leaned across the table, her voice lowered. "Still, you have to admit he is one gorgeous man. And I can tell he's really into you."

How can you tell? Darcy wanted to ask, but she didn't. Because it didn't really matter what someone else thought was going on. The only gauge that counted was what she and Ryder felt. She could assess her own feelings, but the emotions of the other party in a relationship were impossible to plumb. Probably even people who had been together for years had a tough time of it.

So what about her feelings for him? Ryder was gorgeous. And his kisses certainly hadn't been casual pecks on the lips. But they had been thrown together under such odd circumstances. How much of her attraction to him was fueled by fear? If anyone could protect her from this Ice Cold Killer, surely it was a lawman who wore a gun pretty much all the time. And what if she was mistaking his sense of duty to protect her for something more? "I like him," she said. "But it's not as if we've even had a real date." The party had been a good start, but they had been interrupted before they had spent all that much time together.

"You can fix that," Stacy said.

"Fix what?"

"Not having had a date. Ask him out."

"Oh. Well, he's really busy right now."

"He can't work all the time," Stacy said. "He has

to eat, right? Take him to dinner. Or better yet, offer to cook at your place."

Yes, she and Ryder had shared tea and conversation and even soup at her place, but it wasn't a real date. A real date, where she dressed up and cleaned the house and put some effort into a meal, felt like too much just yet. Too intimate and confining.

Maybe a little too reminiscent of her date-turned-nightmare with the man who had raped her.

"Okay, you're not digging that idea," Stacy said. "I can see it on your face. So what about an activity? Maybe something outdoors? Go ice-skating at City Park."

"I don't know how to skate." A broken bone didn't sound very romantic.

"Then something else. You're smart. You can think of something."

"What if he says no?"

"He won't." Stacy pointed her soup spoon at Darcy. "Don't be a coward. And hey, think of it this way—when you're out with a cop, Mr. Ice Cold isn't going to come anywhere near you."

Chapter Fifteen

As the highway closure stretched to its second week, what had been a fun, short-term adventure began to wear on everyone's nerves. Tempers were shorter, complaints were louder and signs on the doors of stores and restaurants warned of limited menus and items no longer available. All the fresh milk and bread in town were gone, though a couple of women were making a killing selling their home-baked loaves, and the local coffee shop had converted more than a few people to almond milk and soy milk lattes. One of the town's two gas stations was out of gas. The city had made the decision to not plow the streets, and people made the best of the situation by breaking out cross-country skis for their commutes.

Darcy figured she had enough fuel to take her through another week. Weather prognosticators were predicting a break in the storms any day now—but they had been saying that for a while.

Four days had passed since Fiona's murder, and though tensions in town were still high, Darcy had stopped flinching every time the door to the clinic opened, and she had stopped looking over her shoulder every few seconds as she drove home in the evening.

"Ryder is here." Stacy made the announcement Wednesday afternoon in a singsong voice reminiscent of a schoolgirl on the playground teasing another girl about her crush.

Darcy finished vaccinating Sage Ryan's tortoise-shell cat and frowned at Stacy. They'd have to have a discussion about interrupting Darcy while she was with a client.

"Do you mean that hunky highway patrolman?" Sage asked as she gathered the cat—Cosmo—into her arms once more. "He's easy enough on the eyes that I might not even mind getting a ticket from him."

"Cosmo should be good for another three years on his rabies vaccine," Darcy said. "He's a nice, healthy cat, though it wouldn't hurt for him to lose a few pounds. I'll ask Stacy to give you our handout on helping cats lose weight."

"Oh, he's just a little pudgy, aren't you, honey?" Sage nuzzled the cat, who looked as if he was only tolerating the attention in hopes it would pay off with a treat. "He's so cute, I can't help but spoil him."

"Try spoiling him with toys and pats instead of treats," Darcy said. "He'll be much better for it in the long run."

"I'll try." She caught Darcy's eye, her cheeks reddening slightly. "And I'm sorry if I said anything out of line about your boyfriend. I promise I didn't mean anything by it."

Darcy opened her mouth to protest that Ryder was not her boyfriend, but the eager look in Sage's eyes changed her mind. No sense providing more fuel for the town gossips.

She followed Sage out to the front. "Now's your chance," Stacy whispered as Darcy passed.

In the waiting room, Ryder rose from the chair he had taken by the door. Dressed in his sharp blue and buff uniform, tall leather boots accenting his strong legs and the leather jacket with the black shearling collar adding to the breadth of his shoulders, he definitely was *easy on the eyes*, as Sage had said. "I didn't mean to interrupt," he said.

"I can give you a few minutes," she said and led the way past Stacy, who didn't even pretend not to stare, into the exam room she'd just exited. "What can I do for you?" she asked, picking up the bottle of spray disinfectant.

"I just wanted to see you, make sure you haven't had any more suspicious customers or disturbances at your home," he said.

"No." She sprayed down the metal exam table. "I promise I'll let you know if anything happens."

"I know." He leaned against the wall, relaxed. "I guess I just wanted to see you. I've been so busy we haven't seen much of each other the past couple of days."

The knowledge that he missed her made her feel a little melted inside. "It's really good to see you, too." She set aside the spray bottle. Her palms were sweating, but it was now or never. "I've been meaning to call you," she said.

"Oh?"

"I wondered if you wanted to go skiing this weekend. I mean, if you're free. I know you're putting in a lot of overtime on the case, but I thought—"

He touched her arm. "I'd love to," he said. "Unless something urgent comes up, I can take a day off. When?"

"Sunday? The office is never open then, and the forecast is for clearing weather."

"Sounds great. I'll pick you up. Is ten o'clock good?"

"Sure." She couldn't seem to stop grinning. "I hope nothing happens to keep you from it. Things have been pretty quiet lately, right?"

"Yeah. But it feels like we're waiting for the other shoe to drop. We know the killer hasn't gone anywhere, because he can't."

"Maybe he's decided to stop killing people."

"That's not usually the way it works with serial killers. I think he's waiting for something."

"Waiting for what?"

"I don't know." He patted her shoulder, then kissed her cheek. "Don't let down your guard," he said. "And I'll see you Sunday morning."

She opened the door of the exam room just wide enough to watch him saunter down the short hallway to the door to the lobby. Now she would be the one waiting, anticipating time alone with Ryder and where that might lead.

THE SNOW THAT had been falling when Ryder awoke Sunday morning had all but stopped by the time he reached Darcy's house, and patches of blue were starting to show through the gray clouds. But Darcy, dressed in a bright yellow and blue parka and snow pants, would have brightened even the dreariest day. Ryder's heart gave a lurch as she walked out to meet him, her smile lighting her face. Oh yeah, he was definitely falling for this woman, though it was harder to read what she felt for him.

At least she looked happy enough to see him today, though maybe it was just the break in the snow that had her smiling. "I'm so relieved to see a change in the weather," she said.

"This was a great idea," he said, opening up the back of the Tahoe and taking the skis she handed to him. "Nothing like getting out in the fresh air to clear away the cobwebs."

"I've been looking forward to a little time off from work," she said, handing him her ski poles.

"I guess it hasn't been easy, handling the practice by yourself," he said. On top of grieving the loss of her friend, she was having to do the work of two people.

"In some ways it's been a blessing." She stepped back and tucked a stray lock of hair beneath her blue stocking cap. "I haven't had too much time to brood. But I haven't had much time off, either. One day soon I need to sit down and draw up a new schedule. I can't keep the office open ten hours a day, six days a week by myself."

"You could bring in another partner," he said.

She wrinkled her nose. "That would be hard to do. The partnership with Kelly worked because we had been such good friends for years. I don't know if I could bring in a stranger. If it were the other way around—if Kelly was the one having to look to replace me—it wouldn't be so hard. She loved meeting new people and she got along with everyone. It takes me a lot longer to warm up to people."

Her eyes met his and he wondered if she was warning him off—or letting him know how privileged he was to be invited closer to her.

She looked away and moved past him to deposit her backpack next to the skis. "I imagine you could use a break, too," she said. "With the roads closed, you're the only state patrol officer in town."

"Yes, though most of my patrol area is closed due to the snow," he said. "Which isn't so bad. It's left me more time to concentrate on the case."

Worry shadowed her face. "You're probably tired of people asking you if you have any suspects."

"I only wish I had a better answer to give than no." He shut the back of the Tahoe. "Maybe a day in the woods will give me a new perspective on the case."

They climbed into the truck and he turned back onto the road. "Where should we go skiing?" she asked. "I know the trails up on Dixon Pass are popular."

Ryder shook his head. "The avalanche danger is too high up there right now. I thought we'd head down valley, to Silver Pick Recreation Area. There are some nice trails through the woods there, sheltered from the wind."

"Kelly and I hiked there this fall," she said. "Right after we moved here. The color in the trees was gorgeous." She settled back in her seat and gazed out the side window. "One of the things I love about living here is there are so many places to go hiking or skiing or just to sit and enjoy nature. The city has plenty of parks, but it's not the same." She glanced at him. "And before Kelly died, I always felt safe out here, even when I was alone. I guess I couldn't imagine any harm could come to me in such a peaceful place."

He tightened his grip on the steering wheel. "I hate that this killer has taken that peace away from you—and from a lot of other people."

"I guess we're naive to think small towns are immune from bad things and bad people," she said. "Or maybe, because crime is so rare in a place like this, it has a bigger impact."

"You would think that a killer hiding in a small population like this would be easier to find," he said. "But that isn't proving to be the case."

She leaned over and squeezed his arm, a gentle, reassuring gesture. "Today let's try not to think about any of that," she said. "Let's just enjoy the day and each other's company."

He covered her hand with his own. "It's a deal."

There were several cars and trucks parked at the recreation area, including a couple of trailers for hauling snow machines. "Snowmobilers have to use the trails on the other side of the road," Ryder said. "We'll probably hear them, but the trails on this side are only for skiers and snowshoers."

They unloaded their skis and packs and set out up an easy groomed trail. After a few strides they fell into a rhythm. The snow had stopped altogether now, only the occasional cascade of white powder sifting down from the trees that lined the trail. The air was sharp with cold, but the sun made it feel less biting and more invigorating.

They had traversed about a half mile up the trail when a loud boom shook the air. Darcy started. "What was that?"

Ryder looked in the direction the explosion had come from. "Sounds like avalanche mitigation up on the pass," he said. "That's good news. The weather forecast must call for clear weather and they're working to get the roads open."

"Oh." Darcy put a hand to her chest. "I guess I knew they used explosives—I just didn't expect for them to sound so loud."

"Sound carries a long way here. And those howitzers they use can be pretty loud."

"Howitzers?" she asked. "As in military weapons?"

"Yeah. They're actually on loan from the army. A lot of the avalanche control crews are ex-military. Their experience with explosives comes in handy. They'll try to bring down as much snow as possible, then get heavy equipment in to haul it off."

"So the highway could be open soon?"

"Maybe as early as tomorrow."

She grinned. "Everyone will be glad to hear it. You wouldn't think a whole town could feel claustrophobic, but it can. And it'll be good to restock all the stores."

"Hopefully the roads will stay clear for all the wedding guests who'll be arriving at the Walker ranch over the next few weeks," Ryder said. "Since some of the party live far away, the family has asked them to stay for an extended visit. They're making kind of a reunion of it, I guess."

"That sounds nice," she said. "It should be a beautiful wedding."

"Would you like to come to the ceremony and reception?" he asked. "I'm allowed to bring a date."

"Oh. Well…"

He cringed inwardly as her voice trailed off. Had he asked too much too soon?

"Yes. I'd love to come with you," she said.

"Good." He faced forward and set out again, though it felt as if his skis scarcely touched the snow.

They paused several times to rest and to take pictures. She snapped a shot of him posed near a snowman someone had built alongside the trail, then they took a selfie in front of a snow-draped blue spruce.

Their destination was a warming hut at the highest point of the trail. They reached it just after noon and raced to kick off their skis and rush inside. The rough-hewn log hut contained a wooden table, several benches and an old black iron woodstove that someone had stoked earlier in the day, so that the warmth wrapped around them like a blanket when they entered.

They peeled off their jackets and Ryder added wood to the stove from the pile just outside the door, while Darcy unpacked a thermos of hot cocoa, two turkey and cheese sandwiches, clementines and peanut butter cookies.

"What a feast," Ryder said as he straddled the bench across from her. He sipped the cocoa, then bit into the sandwich. "Nothing like outdoor exercise to make such a simple meal taste fantastic."

She nodded her agreement, her mouth full of sandwich, laughter in her eyes. A few moments later, when they had both devoured about half the food, she said, "Kelly and I didn't hike this far in the fall. I didn't even know this was up here."

"At the solstice a bunch of people ski or hike up here and have a bonfire," he said. "You should come."

"Maybe I will."

Maybe she would come with him. It felt a little dangerous to think that far ahead, but satisfying, too. Maybe the two of them would have what it took to make it as a couple. This early in their acquaintance, when they were just feeling their way, getting to know each other, anything felt possible.

"Did you make these?" he asked, after taking a bite of a soft, chewy cookie.

She nodded. "I like to bake."

"They're delicious."

They sat side by side on a bench in front of the

hut's one window, a view of the river valley spread out before them. "Road closure or not," he said, "I can't think of anywhere I'd rather be right now than here." He turned to her. "With you."

"Yes," she said. "I feel the same."

There wasn't anything more that needed saying after that. They sat in companionable silence until the cocoa and cookies were gone. "Ready to ski back down?" he asked.

"Yes. I want to stop near the river and take some more pictures of the snow in the trees."

They traveled faster going downhill, racing each other to the flat section of the trail along the river where they stopped and she took more pictures. By the time they started out again, the light was already beginning to fade, the air turning colder and the wind picking up.

When Ryder first heard the snowmobile, he mistook the noise for the wind in the trees. But Darcy, skiing ahead of him, stopped abruptly. "Is that a snowmobile?" she asked. "It sounds like it's heading this way."

"The snow and the trees can distort sound," he said. "All snowmobile traffic is on the other side of the road."

They skied on, but the roar of the machine increased as they emerged into an open area just past the river. "It's probably someone headed to the parking lot," Darcy called over her shoulder.

Ryder started to agree, then saw a flash of light over Darcy's shoulder. The snowmobile emerged from the trees ahead, a single headlight focused on them, a great rooster tail of snow arcing up behind the vehicle.

"What is he doing?" Darcy shouted as the machine bore down on them. She sidestepped off the main trail, but there was nowhere they could go that the snowmobile wouldn't be able to reach. The driver, face obscured by a helmet, leaned over the machine and gunned the engine. He was headed straight for them and showed no sign of veering away or slowing down.

Chapter Sixteen

Darcy stared at the snowmobile charging toward them. The roar of the engine shuddered through her, and the stench of burning diesel stung her nose. *Move!* a voice inside her shouted, but her limbs refused to obey, even as the machine closed the gap between them with alarming speed.

And then she was falling as Ryder slammed into her. They rolled together, a tangle of skis and packs and poles. The snowmobile roared past, a wave of snow washing over them in its wake.

"We've got to get out of these skis!" Ryder shouted. He reached back and slammed his hand onto the release of her skis, then untangled his own legs and pulled her to her feet. The snow off the trail was deep and soft, and she immediately sank to her knees, but Ryder held on to her, keeping her upright. "We have to get into the trees!" he shouted.

She followed his gaze behind them and her stomach turned over as the snowmobile driver made a wide turn and headed back toward them.

"Come on." Ryder tugged on her arm. In his other

hand, he held a gun. Was he really going to shoot the driver? If he did, would that even stop their attacker in time?

The snowmobile bucked forward, and she lurched ahead, as well, Ryder still gripping her arm tightly. They fought their way through heavy snow, every step like walking in a dream, her legs heavy, trapped in the snow. They were in an open field, the line of trees fifty yards or more away, the roar of the snowmobile ever louder as it raced toward them again.

"He's crazy!" she shouted. "How can he hit us without wrecking?"

Ryder shook his head but didn't answer, all his energy divided between breaking a path for them through the drifts and keeping an eye on the snowmobile.

We aren't going to make it, Darcy thought, when she dared to look back and saw the snowmobile only a few dozen yards from them.

The report of Ryder's gun was deafening, and she screamed in spite of herself. The snowmobile veered, then righted. Ryder fired again, and the bullet hit the windscreen, shattering it.

The snowmobile wobbled, then righted itself once more, then the driver turned and headed back the way he had come, away from them.

"I have to go after him," Ryder said. He tucked the pistol into the pocket of his parka. "Can you make it back to the parking lot okay on your own? I'll meet you there."

She nodded, too numb to speak.

He half jogged through the snow, back to the trail and his skis, then took off, kicking hard, making long strides, and was soon out of sight.

She moved much more slowly, her legs leaden. By the time she reached the trail she had begun to shake so hard it took her half a dozen tries to put on both skis. Then she started slowly back toward the parking lot, her movements more shuffle than glide, tears streaming down her face, her mind replaying over and over the sight of that snowmobile bearing down on them.

Ryder met her near the end of the trail. He took her pack from her and skied beside her all the way to the Tahoe, saying nothing. Then he helped her out of her skis and into the truck. "He was gone by the time I got here," he said. "I followed his tracks across the road, but he disappeared into the woods."

"Do you think you hit him when you fired?" she asked, struggling to keep her voice steady.

"No. I hit the machine, but not him."

Neither of them spoke on the drive back to her house. Ryder turned the heat up and Darcy huddled in her seat, unable to get warm. At the house he took her keys and unlocked the door, then she followed him inside.

He closed the door behind them, then pulled her close. They stood with their arms wrapped around each other for a long moment.

"I thought we were going to die," she said, unable to keep her voice from shaking.

He cupped her face in his hands and stared into

her eyes. "We didn't die," he said. "We're going to be okay."

She slid her hands around to the back of his head and pulled his mouth down to hers. She kissed him as if this might be the last chance she ever had of a kiss. Need surged through her—the need to be with him, to feel whole again with him.

She had wasted so much time being cautious, waiting to be sure. Sure of what? What was more sure than how much she wanted him right this minute? What could be more sure than the regret she would have if she didn't seize hold of this moment to live fully?

Ryder returned the kiss with the same ferocity, sliding his hands down to caress her ribs, then bringing them up to cup her breasts. She leaned into him and moved her own hands underneath his sweater, tugging at the knit shirt he wore underneath the wool.

His stomach muscles contracted at her touch, and heat flooded through her. She spread her fingers across his stomach, then slid up to his chest, the soft brush of his chest hair awaking every nerve ending.

He nipped at her jaw, then pulled her fleece top over her head and tossed it aside, followed by her silk long underwear top. Then he began kissing the top of her breasts where they swelled over her bra, and her vision lost focus and she sagged in his arms.

He paused and looked up at her. "How far do you want this to go?" he asked. "Because if you want me to leave, I should probably stop now."

She hugged him more tightly. "Don't leave." Smiling, she reached back and unhooked her bra, then sent it sailing across the room. Out of the corner of her eye, she watched as one of the cats—Pumpkin, she thought—pounced on the lacy toy, which only made her grin more broadly.

The look in Ryder's eyes was worth every bit of the cold chill that made her nipples pucker. He started to reach for her, but she intercepted his hands. "Come on," she said, and led the way to the stairs to the loft.

The stairs were steep and narrow, but they negotiated them in record speed. In the loft Ryder had to duck to avoid hitting his head on the ceiling, but once sprawled on the queen-size bed, his height didn't matter so much. They wasted no time divesting each other of their clothes, then, naked, they slid under the covers.

"This is nice and cozy," he said, pulling her close. "I like the flannel sheets."

"Not as sexy as silk, maybe, but a lot warmer," she agreed.

"Trust me, with you in them, flannel is incredibly sexy." He kissed her, long and deep, while his hands explored her body, learning the shape and feel of her while she did the same with him.

Their leisurely movements gradually became more intense and insistent. Ryder leaned back to study her face. "I probably should have asked this before," he said. "But do you have any protection?"

Smiling, she rolled away from him and opened

the drawer in the bedside table. She handed him the box of condoms.

"This has never been opened," he said. "Did you buy them just for me?"

"That's right," she said. "I've been planning to seduce you for weeks now." Then she grew more serious. "Actually, Kelly gave them to me in a whole box of things when I moved into this place. She said coming here was my chance to get out of my shell and improve my social life. I told her she was being overly optimistic, but maybe I was wrong."

"She was a good friend," Ryder said. "I wish I'd known her better."

"Ha! If you had known her, you never would have looked twice at me," she said. "Men took one look at her blond hair and knockout figure and they couldn't see anything else."

"I prefer brunettes." He took a condom from the box. "And your figure definitely knocks me out."

She sat up and watched him put on the condom, almost dizzy with desire, and then he started to push her back down on the mattress. She stiffened in spite of herself, then tried to force herself to relax. This was Ryder. He wasn't going to hurt her. Everything was going to be fine.

Ryder stilled, then took his hands from her and sat back. "What's wrong?" he asked.

"Nothing's wrong."

"Something's wrong. I felt it. Tell me what I did so I won't do it again."

She looked away, ashamed, and then angry at the

shame. "I just…I don't like someone looming over me. A man. I…I can't relax."

Understanding transformed his face. "I should have realized," he said. "I'm sorry."

"No, it's okay." She sat up, arms hugged across her stomach, fighting back tears. Things had been going so well, and she had to ruin it.

"Hey." He touched her shoulder lightly. "It's okay." He lay down and patted the sheet beside him. "We don't have to rush. We'll take our time and do what feels good for both of us."

Hesitantly, not trusting herself, she lay down beside him again. He stroked her arm, gently, then moved her hand to rest on his chest. "Feel that?" he asked.

She waited, then felt the faint beat of his heart beneath her palm. She looked into his eyes. "Your heartbeat," she said.

He lifted her palm and kissed it, the brush of his tongue sending a jolt of sensation through her. "That's the sound of me, wanting you," he said.

She closed her eyes and he kissed her eyelids, then she was kissing his forehead, his cheek, his ear. They began to move together, desire rebuilding, but somehow deeper, more intense, this time. Facing him, she draped her thigh over his and, eyes open, watching him, she guided him into her. She didn't feel afraid or overwhelmed or anything but aware of her own body and of his—of the tension in his muscles and the heat of her own skin and the wonderful sensation of being filled and fulfilled.

She kept her eyes open as they moved together, and when her climax overtook her, he kissed her, swallowing her cries, and then she saw his face transform with his own moment of release. They held each other, rocking together and murmuring words that weren't really words yet that conveyed a message they both understood.

When at last he eased away from her to dispose of the condom, she let him go reluctantly. When he returned, he pulled her close again, her head cradled on his shoulder, his arm securely around him. The steady beat of his heart lulled her to sleep, the message it sent more powerful than any words.

Chapter Seventeen

Ryder breathed in the perfume of Darcy's hair, and reveled in her softness against him. The comfortable bed in this cozy loft seemed a world apart from the snowy landscape outside where a murderer might lurk. But he could only hide from that world so long, before duty and his conscience drove him to sit up and reach for his clothes.

"You're not leaving, are you?" Darcy shoved up onto one elbow, one bare shoulder exposed, tousled hair falling across her forehead. She looked so alluring, he wondered if he really had the strength to resist the temptation to dive back under the covers with her.

"I'm not leaving," he said, standing and tugging on his jeans. "But I have to call in a report about that snowmobiler." Later he'd have to file a report for his commander, explaining why he had discharged his weapon. "I should have called it in earlier."

"We were both a little distracted," she said, and the heated look that accompanied these words had him aroused and ready all over again.

"I'll, uh, be right back," he said, grabbing a shirt and heading for the stairs.

Three of the four cats met him at the bottom of the steps, studying him with golden eyes, tails twitching. "It's okay," Ryder said, stepping past them. "I'm not the enemy."

He punched in Travis's number and while he waited for the sheriff to answer, he studied the view out the window. The sun was setting, slanting light through the trees and bathing the snow in a rosy glow. It was the kind of scene depicted in paintings and photographs, or on posters with sayings about peace and serenity—not the kind of setting where one expected to encounter danger.

"Ryder? What's up?" Travis's voice betrayed no emotion, only brisk efficiency.

"Darcy and I were skiing over at Silver Pick rec area and a snowmobiler tried to run us down," Ryder said. "I fired off a couple of shots and he fled. I followed, but I lost him on the snowmobile trails on the other side of the road."

"When was this?" Travis asked.

Ryder looked around and spotted the clock on the microwave, which read four thirty. "Around three o'clock," he said.

"And you're just now calling it in?"

"Yes."

Travis paused as if waiting for further explanation, but Ryder didn't intend to offer any. "All right," the sheriff said. "Can you give me a description of the guy, or his snowmobile?"

"It was a Polaris, and one of my shots hit the windscreen and shattered it. The driver was wearing black insulated coveralls and a full helmet, black. That's all I've got."

"Let me make sure I'm clear on this," Travis said. "You and Darcy were on the ski trails, on the east side of the highway, closest to the river, right?"

"Right. We were headed back to the parking lot and were in that open flat, maybe a quarter mile from the parking area. He came straight toward us. We bailed off the trail and tried to make it through the woods, but the snow there is thigh-deep and soft. He missed us his first pass, then turned and came back toward us. That's when I fired on him."

"How many shots?" Travis asked.

"Three. One hit the windscreen and two went wide."

"Hard to hit a moving target like that with a pistol," Travis said. "This doesn't sound like our serial killer. For one thing, running over someone with a snowmobile is a pretty inefficient way to kill someone."

"If he had hit us, chances are he'd have been injured himself," Ryder said. "He probably would have wrecked his machine and could have been thrown off it, too."

"So maybe he wasn't trying to hit you," Travis said. "Maybe he was playing a pretty aggressive game of chicken."

"Maybe," Ryder said. "But he sure looked serious to me."

"Ed Nichols has a Polaris snowmobile," Travis said. "Gage saw it when he interviewed him about his alibi for Kelly's murder."

Nichols. Ryder hadn't focused much attention on the veterinarian after all his alibis had checked out. Clearly, that had been a mistake. "We need to find out what he was doing this afternoon," Ryder said. "And check the windscreen of his snowmobile. Maybe he was the one who ran Darcy off the road that night, too."

"He has an alibi for that evening," Travis said. "He was cooking for a church spaghetti supper."

"It doesn't seem likely we'd be dealing with two different attackers," Ryder said. What could Darcy have done to make herself such a target?

"Question Darcy again," Travis said. "See if she can come up with anyone who might want to get back at her for something. Maybe she failed to save someone's sick dog, or someone disagreed with her bill—it doesn't take much to set some people off."

"I'll do that," Ryder said. "Let me know if you spot any snowmobiles with the windscreens shot out."

He ended the call and turned to find Darcy, wrapped in a pink fleece robe, standing at the bottom of the steps, watching him. "Do you have to go?" she asked.

"No." He pocketed the phone. "I can stay if you want."

"I'd like that." She moved to him and put her arms around him. He kissed the top of her head, wondering how she'd react if he suggested they go back to bed.

"I'd like to take a shower," she said, pulling away from him. "Unfortunately, my shower isn't big enough for two people."

"You go ahead," he said. "I'll clean up when you're done."

She nodded and headed for the bathroom. Once the water was running, Ryder called into his office. His supervisor was out, but he made his report to the duty officer and promised to follow up with the appropriate paperwork. When Darcy emerged from the shower, pink-cheeked, damp hair curling around her throat, he was studying a photo of her standing with an older couple. "Are these your parents?" he asked.

"My mom and her boyfriend." Darcy came to stand beside him. "That was taken the day I graduated from veterinary school."

"Where does she live?" Ryder asked.

"Denver. Though she isn't home that much. She travels a lot. Right now she's in China, I think. Or India?" She frowned. "It's hard to keep up. We're not close."

"I'm sorry," he said and meant it. Though he didn't see them often, he had always felt embraced by his own family.

"It's okay," she said.

"Where is your father?" he asked.

"I have no idea. He and my mother divorced when I was six months old. I never knew him."

His instinct was to tell her how sad this was, but

clearly, she didn't want any sympathy. "What about your family?" she asked.

"My mom and dad are in Cheyenne," he said. "I have a brother in Seattle and a sister in Denver. We're all pretty close."

"That's nice." She patted his arm. "The shower is all yours."

When he emerged from the shower—which, in keeping with everything else in the house, was tiny—she handed him a glass of wine. "I don't have anything stronger in the house," she said. "I figured we could both use it."

She sat on the sofa, legs curled up beneath her robe, and he moved aside a couple of throw pillows and sat beside her, his arm around her shoulders. She snuggled close. "What a day, huh?" she said.

He stroked her shoulder. "Are you okay?"

"Better." She sipped the wine, then set the glass on the low table in front of them. "I can't promise I won't have nightmares about that snowmobile headed straight for us. I mean, it was scary when that guy ran me off the road, but this was worse. I felt so vulnerable, out there in the open. And he seemed closer, without a vehicle around him. The attack seemed so much more personal." She shuddered, and he set aside his glass to wrap his other arm around her.

They were both silent for a long moment. Ryder wondered if she was crying, but when she looked up at him, her eyes were dry. "Why is someone trying to kill me?" she asked.

"Kill you—or frighten you badly," Ryder said.

He leaned forward and handed her her wineglass and picked up his own. "I know I've asked you this before, but can you think of anyone who might want to hurt you? A client or someone who wanted to rent this place and you beat them to it? Anything like that?"

She shook her head. "I've thought and thought and there isn't anyone."

"We checked on Jay Leverett," he said, not missing how she stiffened at the mention of the name.

"Oh?" she asked.

"He was released from prison two months ago. We're still trying to find out where he went after that."

"I'm sure I would recognize him if he was here in Eagle Mountain," she said. She set her now-empty wineglass aside and half turned to face Ryder. "Why would he come after me now—after all this time? It's been six years since he raped me, and I wasn't the first woman he had hurt—or the only one. Mine wasn't even the crime he was sentenced for—he was caught when he broke into a girls' dorm and attacked one of the women there. Why would he come after me?"

"What he did to you before didn't make sense, either," Ryder said. "And this may have nothing to do with him. We just need to be sure."

"Did whoever is after me kill Kelly and Christy and Fiona, too?" she asked.

"We don't know," Ryder said. "Your attacker could be someone different. As far as we know,

Kelly and the others were never pursued prior to their deaths."

"How did I get to be so lucky?" She tried to smile but failed, and her voice shook.

He took both her hands in his—they were ice cold. "We can find you a safe place to stay until we've tracked this guy down," he said. "Travis's family probably has room at their ranch—or you could stay with me. My place isn't much, but you'd be safe there."

She nodded. "Maybe it's time for something like that," she said. "I mean, I don't want to be stupid about this—I just hate being chased out of my own home."

"I understand." He admired her independence, but was relieved she was smart enough to accept help. "My place isn't set up for cats, but if you tell me what you need…"

"I think I'll leave them here," she said. "I can come by and check on them every day."

"Do you want me to call Travis and have him ask his parents if you can stay with them, or are you comfortable moving in with me?"

"I'll stay with you." She leaned toward him once more, her hands on his shoulders. "I think I can trust you."

He knew how much those words meant, coming from her. He pulled her close. "We don't have to be in any hurry," he said. "What would you think if I spent the night here tonight?"

A slow smile spread across her lips. "I think that's

a very good idea," she whispered and kissed him, a soft, deep kiss that hinted at much more to come.

HALF OF DARCY'S clients canceled their appointments the next day. The highway had opened at last, and everyone was anxious to drive over the pass to do shopping and run errands. A steady stream of delivery trucks flowed into town. The prospect of new supplies, along with the abundant sunshine, had everyone in a jubilant mood.

"If I call the patients who still have appointments today and convince them to come in early, do you think we could close up ahead of schedule?" Stacy asked after yet another client called to move their appointment to another day. "I'd really like to get over to Junction and do some shopping."

"That sounds like a good idea," Darcy said.

"You could come with me, if you like."

"Thanks, but I've got plenty to keep me busy here." She and Ryder had agreed that she would head back to her place after work, pack up whatever she thought she needed for the next few days, make sure the cats were settled, then drive over to his house.

It's only temporary, she reminded herself. *It's not as if we're really moving in together.* After all, they had known each other only a few days, even though it felt as if he already knew her better than anyone ever had. He had learned to read her moods and anticipate her thoughts, attuned to her in a way that was both touching and awe-inspiring.

When they reopened the office after lunch, Darcy

was surprised to find Ken waiting outside the clinic. "What can we do for you?" Stacy asked as she waited for Darcy to unlock the door. "Are you overdue for your rabies shot?"

"Very funny." He followed them into the clinic. "I just stopped by to see how you're doing," he said to Darcy.

"I'm fine." Had word somehow gotten out about her encounter with the homicidal snowmobiler the day before?

"Why wouldn't she be fine?" Stacy asked.

Ken glared at her. "Don't you have work to do?"

"It's much more fun to annoy you."

Ken turned his back on her. "The sheriff's department and that highway patrolman haven't done anything to stop this Ice Cold Killer. Everyone is wondering who he's going to kill next."

"The local law enforcement officers are working very hard to try to stop the killer," Darcy said.

"But they aren't getting anywhere, are they? They don't have any suspects, do they?" He stared at her as if expecting an answer.

"I wouldn't know," she said.

"I thought you might, since you and that highway patrolman are so cozy."

He looked as if he expected her to confirm or deny this. She did neither. She certainly wasn't going to tell Ken she was moving in with Ryder. She had decided not to share their plans with anyone. Not because she was ashamed, but because she and Ryder had agreed the fewer people who knew where she was, the safer she would be.

She took her white coat from its peg and put it on. "Thanks for stopping by," she said. "I have to get ready to see my afternoon patients."

"I know the female teachers at my school are terrified," he continued. "The male teachers have agreed to walk them to their cars, kind of like bodyguards."

"That's very thoughtful of you," Darcy said.

"You should do something like that here," he said.

"I'm being careful."

"Now that the highway is open, maybe the killer will take the opportunity to get out of here," Stacy said. "Maybe he's already gone."

"I guess that would be good," Ken said.

"I'd rather see him caught and stopped," Darcy said. "I hate to think of him moving on to somewhere else to kill more women."

"Now that the road is open, maybe they'll get some experts in who can track him down," Ken said.

Darcy resisted the impulse to defend Ryder. She sensed Ken was only trying to bait her, and she wasn't going to waste energy sparring with him.

He shifted his weight to his other hip, apparently prepared to stay until she ordered him away. "I guess now that the road is open, Kelly's parents will be coming to clear her things out of the duplex," he said.

"I guess so." She frowned, thinking of all the clinic supplies in the garage. "I'll need to clear out the garage," she said. "And find some place to store all that stuff here."

"Why don't you just move in, instead?" Ken asked. "My landlord would be happy to find a renter so easily. You'd be closer to work and town and you could still use the garage for storage."

"I like the place where I am now," she said.

"Sure. But it's not safe for you out there. You're way too vulnerable without other people around. If you lived in town, I'd be right next door, and there are other neighbors nearby."

She couldn't tell him that having him right on the other side of her living room wall wasn't something she looked forward to. "I'll be fine. And now I really do need to get ready for my patients." Not waiting for an answer, she turned and walked into the back room, closing the door from the waiting room firmly behind her.

A few moments later Stacy joined her in the section of the big back room they used as their in-house laboratory, where Darcy was unpacking a new supply of blood collection tubes. "Poor Ken," Stacy said. "He's still crazy about you. He can't get over losing you."

"He never had me to lose," Darcy said. "We only went out three times." And she had only agreed to the third date so that she could tell him to his face that she didn't have romantic feelings for him and didn't believe she ever would. She had tried to let him down gently, but she had also been clear that she didn't want to date him again.

"Still, I feel sorry for him," Stacy said. "He's one of these guys who tries too hard."

"Then you date him."

"I'm married, remember?" She leaned back against the lab table. "I didn't say I thought you ought to go out with him. Ryder is a much better guy for you." She grinned. "How did your date go yesterday?"

"It went…well."

"Uh-oh. I distinctly heard a 'but' in there. What happened?"

Darcy pushed aside the half-empty box of tubes. "You can't tell anyone, okay?"

"Cross my heart." She made an X across her chest with her forefinger.

"We had a great time," Darcy said. "It was a beautiful day and we skied up to the warming hut at the top of the hill and had lunch."

Stacy looked disappointed. "That's not a 'but.'"

"I'm getting to the bad part." She took a deep breath. Better to just come out with it. "On the way back down, a guy on a snowmobile tried to run us over."

"I thought snowmobiles weren't allowed on the ski trails," Stacy said.

"They're not. But he deliberately tried to kill us. When he missed the first time, he turned around and headed for us again."

"Sheesh, woman! What is with you and guys trying to run you down?" She touched Darcy's arm. "Sorry. I wasn't trying to be insensitive. Are you okay?"

Darcy nodded. "I was terrified at the time. But

Ryder pulled his gun and shot at the guy and he raced off. Ryder tried to follow, but he got away."

"Do you have any idea who it was?"

"No. He was wearing a full helmet with a visor. There was no way to know."

The bells on the front door announced the arrival of their first afternoon patient. A dog's insistent bark confirmed this. "That will be Judy Ericson and Tippy," Stacy said. She squeezed Darcy's arm. "I'm so glad you're okay. And I hope they find out who it was."

"One of Ryder's bullets hit the windshield of the snowmobile," Darcy said. "He's hoping that will help him find the guy."

"Ryder should talk to Bud O'Brien—he rents snowmobiles out of his garage," Stacy said. "If this maniac was a tourist who's stuck here, he might not have his own snowmobile. He'd have to rent one."

"That's a great idea. I'll pass it on."

Stacy headed to the door, but stopped before she opened it and turned to face Darcy again. "I think I agree with Ken on this one—you shouldn't be out at your place by yourself. You're welcome to stay with me and Bill."

"I'll be fine," Darcy said. "I promise."

Stacy nodded. "At least you have one thing going for you," she said.

"What's that?"

"You've got Ryder on your side. That's worth a lot."

Chapter Eighteen

"Now that the highway is open, the Colorado Bureau of Investigation is sending in its own team to investigate the murders," Ryder told Travis when they met at the sheriff's department Monday morning.

"So I hear," Travis said. "Good luck to them. So far we don't have a lot to go on."

"When I spoke with my boss this morning, he told me to deliver the physical evidence to the state lab in Junction as soon as possible," Ryder said. "I had to tell him we didn't have any physical evidence—no blood, no hair or fibers, no prints."

"I checked with Ed Nichols about his whereabouts yesterday afternoon," Travis said. "He says he was home with his wife, watching television."

"That's a hard alibi to disprove if his wife backs him up," Ryder said. "What about the snowmobile?"

"It wasn't there," Travis said. "He said it's at O'Brien's Garage, waiting on a part."

"A new windscreen?"

"I don't know. O'Brien's was closed when I went

by there, and the phone goes to an answering machine. Bud didn't answer his home phone, either."

"I'll go by his house," Ryder said. "He'll want as much as anyone to get to the bottom of this. But first, I want to interview Tim and Alex again. I want to see what they were up to yesterday afternoon."

"There was only one man on that snowmobile," Travis said.

"Maybe it was one of them—maybe it wasn't," Ryder said.

"The problem I have is with motive," Travis said. "Why go after Darcy?"

Gage joined them. "I heard about what happened yesterday," Gage said. "Is Darcy okay?"

"She's holding up," Ryder said. He turned to Travis once more. "She tried again to think of someone who might have a grudge against her and came up with nothing." He hesitated. He wanted to honor the trust Darcy had placed in him by revealing her past, but he couldn't keep information pertaining to the case from Travis. "She does have an ex-boyfriend who went to jail after kidnapping and raping her," he said. "It happened six years ago, and he was released from prison two months ago, after serving time for another crime. I received a report about him yesterday—no current address. But Darcy is sure she hasn't seen him here in town."

"He could have avoided her," Travis said. "He wouldn't want her to know he was behind the attacks."

"Right. His name is Jay Leverett," Ryder said.

"I gave his description to the other officers, and it's on your desk."

"We'll be on the lookout for him," Travis said. He turned to Gage. "I need you to contact Bud O'Brien," he said. "Find out why Ed Nichols's snowmobile is at his garage, how long it's been there and if it has a damaged windscreen."

"Will do," Gage said.

Travis turned back to Ryder. "I'll go with you to interview Tim and Alex."

"We should try to get Darcy into a safe house," Travis said when he and Ryder were in Travis's cruiser. "I can make some calls…"

"She'll never go for that," Ryder said. "And she has a business to run here in town."

"I can try to run extra patrols out her way, but I don't really have the personnel," Travis said.

"It's okay. I talked her into moving in with me."

Travis glanced at him, one eyebrow quirked, but all he said was, "All right, then."

No vehicles were parked in the driveway at the cabin where Alex and Tim were staying, and no one answered Travis's knock. "Maybe they left town already," Ryder said. He scanned the snow-covered yard. A black plastic trash can on rollers sat against the house, next to a half cord of firewood. No snowmobile.

Travis walked along the narrow front porch and peered into a window. "If they did, they left behind most of their stuff," he said.

Ryder cupped his hands against the windowpane

and studied the clothing, shoes, beer cans, half-empty bags of chips and video game controllers scattered across the sofa and coffee table. "Yeah, it doesn't look like they went back to Denver yet," he agreed.

The two men returned to Travis's cruiser. "What now?" Ryder asked.

"I need to run up to my folks' ranch," Travis said. "I've got a couple of guests that are supposed to arrive now that the road is open. One of them is the caterer and I want to make sure she has everything she needs."

"Rainey and Doug Whittington aren't doing the food for the wedding?"

"They wanted to, but this woman is a friend of Lacy's. It was important to her to have her do the wedding and I wasn't going to argue. And Rainey is always complaining about how much work all the wedding guests are for her, so she should appreciate the help."

Rainey struck Ryder as the type who wouldn't want to share her kitchen with anyone, but he kept that opinion to himself. "Speaking of the Whittingtons, does Doug have a snowmobile?" he asked.

"He doesn't own one," Travis said. "But he certainly has access to several. I'll check on that while I'm up there."

Ryder glanced back toward the house. "I'll swing by here later and try to catch these two—try to find out what their plans are." He started to mention the lack of a snowmobile but was interrupted by the insistent beeping from his shoulder-mounted radio.

"Report to Dixon Pass for one-vehicle accident. Vehicle is blocking the road."

"Guess that means the pass is closed again," Travis said. "It's going to be a long winter."

Ryder nodded. "It's already too long for me."

DARCY WAVED GOODBYE to Stacy and headed for the Green Monster. As long as she still had the truck, she might as well move the boxes from Kelly's garage to the office. She told herself she was being practical, tackling the job now, and tried to ignore the voice in the back of her head that said she was only delaying taking her things to Ryder's house.

Not that she wasn't looking forward to spending more time with him—she definitely was. And she knew she would be much safer with what amounted to her own personal bodyguard. But moving in with a man, even temporarily, was a big step. One she wasn't sure she was ready to take. She certainly wouldn't be doing this now when they had known each other so little time, if circumstances—or rather, a deranged man who was possibly a killer—hadn't forced her hand.

She pulled into the driveway of the duplex, relieved to see no sign of Ken or his truck. The house looked even more neglected when she stepped inside, the air stale, the furniture lightly covered with dust. She made her way to the garage and opened the automatic door from the inside, then set about transferring boxes to the back of the truck. Fortunately, none of the cartons was particularly heavy, though by the time she had filled the truck bed, she felt as if she had had a workout. She slammed the tailgate shut and surveyed the full bed. She had managed to get everything in.

Something cold kissed her cheek and she looked up into a flurry of gently falling white flakes. More snow felt like an insult at this point, but she reminded herself this was what winter in the mountains was all about. She needed to get used to it.

She went back inside to shut the garage door, but stopped just inside the doorway. This might be the last time she was ever in this house—a place that held so many memories. She and Kelly had spent countless evenings here, drinking wine and eating pizza, binge-watching television or planning the next steps for the veterinary practice. She could almost see her friend, seated in the corner of the sofa, a bowl of popcorn in her lap, her hair pulled up in a messy ponytail, head thrown back, laughing. The memory made her smile, even as unshed tears pinched at her throat.

From the living room she walked down a short hallway to the master bedroom, the bed unmade as it almost always was, clothes thrown over a chair, shoes discarded just inside the doorway. She bent and picked up a red high heel. Kelly loved shoes, and was always encouraging Darcy to go for prettier, sexier footwear. She understood Darcy had no desire to call attention to herself with provocative clothing, but she tried to do whatever she could to help her friend get over the fear behind those inhibitions.

The two had met only a few months after Darcy's rape. Kelly had come in late to a class and taken the vacant seat next to Darcy. In the next five minutes she had borrowed a pen, some notepaper, shared half a carrot cake muffin and invited Darcy to have lunch with her. Swept along in what she later thought of as Hurricane Kelly, Darcy had found herself befriended by this vibrant, fearless woman. Though their personalities were so different, they bonded quickly. When Kelly learned about Darcy's traumatic experience, she had become her biggest cheerleader and defender.

When she had first visited Darcy's apartment and seen the array of locks on the door—and learned that Darcy left the lights on all night, even though it made it hard to sleep—she had invited Darcy to move in with her. Gradually, Darcy had gained the confidence to sleep without the lights on. Kelly had found a therapist who specialized in helping rape victims, and had accompanied Darcy to the first appointment.

Though Kelly had been nurturing and protective, she had refused to let Darcy become dependent on her. At every turn, Kelly encouraged Darcy to try new things, take new risks and expand her boundaries. She could be overbearing, and the two friends had had their share of disagreements. But in the end Kelly had saved her. It grieved Darcy beyond words that she hadn't been able to save her friend.

She shook her head, set the shoe on the dresser and left the room. Time to get on with it. As she passed through the kitchen on her way to the garage, she decided to check Kelly's pantry for more cat food. No sense letting it go to waste. She found an unopened bag of dry food, and half a dozen cans, as well as a brand-new catnip mouse. The cats would appreciate a new toy, and it would help assuage her guilt at abandoning them while she stayed with Ryder.

She was searching for a bag to put the food in, humming to herself, when pain jolted her. The cat food cans tumbled from her arms and rolled across the kitchen floor as blackness overtook her.

Chapter Nineteen

The eighteen-wheeler had slid sideways across the highway near the top of Dixon Pass, until the back wheels of the trailer slipped off the edge, while the rest of the truck sprawled across both lanes. The driver had somehow managed to stop, and gravity and one large boulder had prevented the rig from sliding farther. The road was at its narrowest here, with almost no shoulders and no guardrails. The driver, who had bailed out of the cab, now stood in the shelter of a rock overhang, staring through a curtain of falling snow, hands shoved in the pockets of his leather coat, while they waited for a wrecker to come and winch the rig all the way back onto the road.

"The wrecker should be here in about ten minutes," Ryder told the driver, ending the call from his dispatcher. "What are you hauling?"

"Insulation." He wiped his hand across his face. "Yesterday I had a load of bottled water. All those heavy bottles probably would have shifted and taken me on over the side." His hand shook as he returned it to his pocket.

"You got off lucky," Ryder said.

"Yeah. I guess so."

Ryder moved away and, shoulders hunched against the falling snow, hit the button to call Darcy. He needed to let her know he was going to be late. She should let herself into the house with the key he had given her and make herself at home. Even though they had both agreed this stay would only be temporary, he wanted her to feel she could treat his place as her own. He let the call ring, then frowned as it went to voice mail. Maybe she was with a late patient and couldn't be interrupted. He left a message and stowed the phone again as a man in a puffy red coat and a fur hat strode toward him through the falling flakes.

"How much longer is the road going to be closed?" the man asked in the tone of someone who is much too busy to be stalled by petty annoyances.

"Another hour at least," Ryder said. "Maybe more. It depends on how long it takes to move the truck."

"You people need to do a better job of keeping the highway open," the man said. "Isn't that what we're paying you for?"

"I'm charged with keeping the public safe," Ryder said.

"They should keep these big rigs off the road when the weather is like this," the man said. "They're always causing trouble."

Ryder could have pointed out that passenger cars

had more accidents than trucks, but decided not to waste his breath. "A wrecker is on the way to deal with this truck," he said. "If you don't want to wait, you can turn around."

"I can't turn around," he said. "I have business in Eagle Mountain."

"Then you'll need to go back to your vehicle and wait."

The man wanted to argue, Ryder could tell, but a stern look from Ryder suppressed the urge. He turned and stalked back toward his SUV. Ryder didn't even give in to the urge to laugh when he slipped on the icy pavement and almost fell.

Ryder's phone rang and he took the call from Travis. "I checked at the ranch and none of our snow machines are damaged," Travis said. "And Rainey swears Doug was helping her in the kitchen all yesterday afternoon. I haven't heard yet from Gage about Ed's snowmobile."

"Thanks for checking," Ryder said. "Did your caterer make it?"

"She called Lacy a little while ago and told her she's stuck in traffic. Apparently, a wreck has the highway closed again."

"Yeah. We're going to get it cleared away in an hour or two." He looked up at the gently falling snow. "I'm hoping the highway department can keep it open. Looks like we've got more snow."

"I'll try to get by Alex and Tim's place tomorrow to talk to them," Travis said.

"I'll do it on my way home this afternoon," Ryder

said. "It's on my way." He really wanted to talk to those two before they slipped out of town.

Two hours later the wrecker had winched the eighteen-wheeler to safety. The driver, and all the cars that had piled up behind him, were safely on their way, and a Colorado Department of Transportation plow trailed along behind them, pushing aside the six inches of snow that had accumulated on the roadway. As long as the plows kept running and no avalanche chutes filled and dumped their loads on the highway, things would flow smoothly.

Ryder turned traffic patrol over to a fellow officer and headed back into Eagle Mountain. He tried Darcy's phone again—still no answer. Maybe she'd forgotten to charge it, or was simply too busy to answer it, he told himself. He resisted the urge to drive straight to his house, hoping to find her there, and stuck with his plan of interviewing Tim and Alex.

But first, he had to stop for gas. He was fueling the Tahoe when a red Jeep pulled in alongside him. "Hello, Ryder," Stacy said.

"Hi, Stacy," he said. "You're getting off work a little late, aren't you?"

"Oh, I've been off hours," she said, getting out of her car and walking around to the pump. "We closed up early and I went into Junction to do some shopping. I made it back just before the road closed again, but then I had more errands to run here in town." She indicated the back of the Jeep, which was piled high with bags and boxes. "It's been a while."

If she had closed the clinic early, then Darcy probably hadn't been with a patient when he called earlier. So why wasn't she answering her phone? "Do you know where Darcy headed after you closed?" he asked.

"She said she had things to do," Stacy said.

"Did she say what?"

"Easy there, officer. Is something wrong?"

He reined in his anxiety. "I've tried to call her a couple of times and she isn't answering."

Stacy frowned. "That isn't like her. She said something earlier about needing to get all the clinic supplies out of Kelly's duplex. I guess now that the highway is open again, Kelly's parents want to come and clean it out. Maybe she decided to take care of that."

Maybe so. Though that still didn't explain why she hadn't answered his calls.

He headed for Tim's aunt's cabin next, determined to get that interview out of the way. The gray Toyota with the dent in the front quarter-panel sat parked in the driveway of the cabin, a frosting of snow obscuring the windows. Ryder parked his Tahoe behind the Toyota and made his way up the unshoveled walk to the vehicle. A deep indentation ran the length of the driver's side front quarter-panel, the metal gouged as if by a sharp object.

Ryder straightened and made his way to the front door. Alex answered his knock, dressed in black long underwear pants and top. "Hey," he said. "What you need?"

"Can I come in?" Ryder asked. "I need to ask a few questions."

Alex shrugged. "I guess so." He held the door open.

Tim was sprawled across the sofa, wearing green-and-black-check flannel pants and a Colorado State University sweatshirt, a video game controller in his hands. He sat up and frowned at Ryder. "What do you want?"

"The highway is open," Ryder said, stepping around a pile of climbing gear—ropes and packs and shoes. "I figured the two of you would be headed back to Denver."

"We took advantage of the great weather to go climbing." Alex sat on the end of the sofa and picked up a beer from the coffee table. "We don't have to be back in class until the end of the month, anyway."

"What do you care?" Tim asked, his attention on the television screen, which was displaying a video game that seemed to revolve around road racing.

"What did the two of you do Sunday?" Ryder asked.

"What did we do Sunday?" Tim asked Alex.

"We went climbing." Alex sipped the beer.

"Where did you go?" Ryder asked.

"Those cliffs over behind the park," Alex said. "And before you ask if anyone saw us, yeah, they did. Two women. We went out with them that night."

"I'll need their names and contact information," Ryder said.

"Why?" Tim asked. "Did another woman get iced?" He laughed, as if amused by his joke.

"Have you visited Silver Pick Recreation Area while you've been in town?" Ryder asked.

"We checked it out," Alex said. "We didn't see any good climbing."

"Good snowmobile trails," Ryder said.

"We talked about renting a couple of machines," Tim said. "Too expensive. Climbing's free."

"Since when are you concerned about us having a good time?" Alex asked.

"We're looking for a snowmobiler who threatened a couple of people out at Silver Pick Sunday afternoon. He tried to run them down with his snowmobile."

"It wasn't us," Alex said.

"Maybe it was the same idiot who smashed my truck," Tim said.

"Yeah," Alex said. "What are you doing about trying to find that guy?"

"I don't think there's a guy to find," Ryder said.

"What?" Tim sat up straight. "Are you calling us liars?"

"I took another look at that dent on your truck," Ryder said. "It's too low to the ground to have been made by another car. And too sharp."

"It is not," Tim said.

"The more I think about it, the more it looks like it was made by those big chunks of granite that edge the parking lot near the ice climbing area out on County Road Fourteen," Ryder said. "It's easy enough to do—don't pay attention to what you're doing and you can run into one of them, scrape the heck out of your car."

"You can't prove it," Tim said.

"I'll bet if I went out there, I'd find paint from your truck on one of the rocks," Ryder said.

Tim and Alex exchanged looks. "Why would we bother making up a story and getting the police involved if it wasn't true?" Alex asked.

"If someone else caused the damage to your car, maybe you thought you could get your insurance to pay for it under your uninsured motorist coverage," Ryder said. "It works like that in other states—for instance, in Texas, where you said you were from. But it doesn't work that way in Colorado. In Colorado you have to have collision coverage in order for the insurance to pay."

"No way!" Tim looked at Alex. "You told me we could get the insurance company to pay. Now what am I going to do?"

Alex ignored his friend. He looked at Ryder. "If you think you can prove something, have at it. Otherwise, why don't you leave us alone?"

"I'll leave for now," Ryder said. "But you'll be hearing from me again." Tomorrow he would go to the parking lot and try to find the rock they had hit. Filing a false report to a peace officer was at best a misdemeanor, but the charge would be a hassle for the two young men, and having to deal with it might teach them a lesson.

From the cabin to the place Ryder rented was only

a short drive. His heart sank when he saw that the driveway was empty. He hurried into the house, hoping to see some sign that Darcy had been there, but everything was just as he had left it. No suitcases or bags or any of Darcy's belongings. He pulled out his phone and dialed her number again. Still no answer. What was going on?

DARCY WOKE TO familiar surroundings, sure she was in her own bed, but with the terrible knowledge that something was very wrong. When she tried to sit up, she discovered that her hands were tied to the headboard, and her ankles were bound together. She began to shake with terror, almost overwhelmed with the memory of another time when she had been tied to a bed, unable to escape her tormentor.

"Don't struggle now. You don't want to hurt yourself." Ken leaned over her, his smile looking to her eyes like a horrible grimace.

"What are you doing?" she asked. The memory of being in Kelly's kitchen flooded back. She had been looking at cat food and the next thing she knew, she woke up here. "Did you hit me on the head?"

"It was for your own good," Ken said. "If you had listened to me when I offered to let you move in with me, it wouldn't have been necessary."

"Let me go!" She struggled against the ropes that held her. The bed shook and creaked with her efforts, but she remained trapped.

"No, I can't do that," Ken said. "If I do that, you'll only call the sheriff, or that state trooper, Ryder.

Then I'd have to leave and you'd be here all alone and unprotected."

"I don't need protection," she said.

"But you do. There's a serial killer in town who's murdering young women just like you. You don't want to be his next victim, do you?"

She stared at him, searching for signs that he had lost his mind. He looked perfectly ordinary and sane. Except every word he uttered chilled her to the core.

He sat on the side of the bed, the mattress dipping toward her. "What are you doing?" she asked, trying to inch away from him.

He put his hand on her leg. "I'm going to protect you."

"Did you kill Kelly and those other women?" she asked. If he was the murderer, was confronting him this way a mistake? But she had to know.

His hand on her leg tightened. "Is that what you think of me?" he asked. "That I'm a killer? A man who hates women?" He slid his hand up her leg. "I love women. I love you. I've loved you since the first time I saw you with Kelly. I kept waiting for you to see it, but you couldn't. Or you wouldn't." His fingers closed around her thigh, digging deep.

"Stop!" She tried to squirm out of his grasp. "You're hurting me."

"I decided I had to do something to wake you up," he said, continuing to massage her thigh painfully. "To make you see how much I love you."

"If you loved me, you wouldn't frighten me this way," she said. "You wouldn't hurt me."

"I won't hurt you." He leaned over her, his voice coaxing. "In fact, I'm going to show you how gentle I can be." He moved his hand to the waistband of her slacks.

She closed her eyes and swallowed down a scream. There was no one to hear her, and if she screamed, she might give in to the panic that clawed at her. Hysterics wouldn't help her. She had to hang on. She had survived before, and she would survive again.

How long before Ryder came looking for her? He would be expecting her at his house, but what if he had to work late? She had no idea what time it was, though the window at the end of the loft showed only blackness. If could be seven o'clock or it could be midnight—she couldn't tell.

But no matter the hour, she had to find a way out of this situation. So far Ken hadn't threatened her with a gun. As far as she knew, he didn't own one. He was counting on his size and strength to overpower her, and so far it was working for him, but she had to find some advantage and figure out a way to use it against him.

"You need to untie me," she said, surprised at how calm she sounded. "I can't relax and…and I can't focus on you if I'm tied up."

"You don't like being tied up?" He looked genuinely puzzled. "I thought it would be fun." He grinned. "A little kinky."

She swallowed nausea. "I just…I want to put my arms around you," she said.

He sat back, searching her face. "You won't try to fight me?"

"Of course not," she lied.

"I'll untie your hands," he said and leaned forward to do so. "But I'll leave your feet the way they are. I don't want you running away."

She forced herself to remain still while he fumbled with the knots at her wrists. "Maybe you need a knife," she said.

"Good idea." He stood, then winked at her. "Don't go away. I'll be right back."

"I'll be waiting." Saying the words made her feel sick to her stomach. But she would be waiting when he returned with the knife—then she would do everything to get her hands on that blade. He thought she was passive, but he would learn she was a fighter.

Chapter Twenty

The parking lot of the veterinary clinic was empty, the only tracks in the smooth coating of snow the fresh ones made by Ryder's Tahoe. He tried the door, anyway, and peered through the glass. A single light behind the front desk illuminated the empty counter. The only sound was the crunch of his own boots on the snow.

He tried Darcy's phone again, and this time the call went straight to voice mail. He hung up without leaving a message, stomach churning. Where was she?

He headed for her house, but since Kelly's duplex was on the way, decided to swing by there first. Stacy had mentioned that Darcy had planned to pick up some supplies from there. Maybe she had gotten distracted, or the task took more time than he would have thought. But even as he thought these things, instinct told him something was wrong.

The driveway to the duplex was vacant, and no lights shone from either half. The snow was falling harder now, filling in Ryder's tracks on the walkway to the door within minutes of his passing. He knocked on Kelly's door, then tried the knob. It was locked. With a growing sense of urgency, he moved to Ken's door and pounded on it. "Ken, it's Ryder! I need to talk to you."

He turned and headed back across the porch and up the walk toward his Tahoe. But a dark bulk along the side of the duplex caught his eye. He unclipped the flashlight from his utility belt and shone it over a tarped snowmobile. Heart pounding, he stepped through the deepening snow to the snowmobile and unhooked the bungie cord that held the tarp in place.

His flashlight illuminated first the Polaris emblem. Then he arced the beam upward to the spiderweb of cracks in the windscreen that spread out from the neat, round bullet hole.

KEN CUT THE plastic ties that had bound Darcy's wrists and laid the knife on the floor beside the bed. She stretched her arms out in front of her, wincing at the pain, and struggled to sit up. Ken pushed her back onto the bed with one hand, reaching for the fly of his jeans with the other.

"Wait," she cried, squirming into a sitting position. She forced a smile to her trembling lips. "Let's talk a little bit first. You know—get in the mood."

He frowned but moved his hand away from his fly. "What do you want to talk about?"

"Were you the one on the snowmobile on the ski trail at Silver Pick Sunday afternoon?"

"What about it?"

"I just wondered." She swallowed, trying to force some saliva from her dry mouth. "I figure you were trying to show me how dangerous it was," she said. "How much I need to depend on you to protect me."

His expression lightened. "That's it." He sat beside her and took her hand in his. "I didn't want to frighten you, but I had to make you see the danger you were in. I did it to protect you."

"And were you the one who ran me off Silverthorne Road?" she asked. "You pretended to be that woman with the hurt mastiff?"

He laughed. "That was pretty clever, wasn't it?" He leaned closer. "If only you weren't so stubborn. You would have saved us all so much trouble if you had accepted my help from the first."

She pushed him gently away, trying hard to hide her revulsion and fear. "Did you try to break in to this place, the night Kelly was killed?"

He frowned. "No. I wouldn't do something like that."

Hitting her over the head and kidnapping her, not to mention threatening her with both a truck and a snowmobile, apparently weren't as bad as jimmying a lock? But she believed him when he said he hadn't tried to break in that night. But was he the killer?

Ken forced his lips onto hers and slid his hands under her sweater. Her stomach churned and she wondered if it was possible to vomit from fear. Would that be enough to scare him off?

"I'm ready now." He stood and, so quickly she hardly registered what was happening, shoved his jeans down. She reacted instinctively, drawing up her legs, ankles still bound together, and shoving hard against his chest. He stumbled back and she dove for the floor, grabbing for the knife.

He straddled her, hands around her throat, choking her, as she felt blindly for the knife, which had slid under the bed. Her fingers closed around the handle, as he shoved his knee into her back, forcing her flat onto the floor. And all the while his hands continued to squeeze until her vision fogged and she felt herself slipping away.

A mighty crash shook the whole house, and the pressure on her throat lessened. "What the—"

"Darcy!" Ryder's shout was followed by pounding footsteps as he vaulted up the stairs.

His weight still grinding her into the floor, Ken swiveled to face the entrance to the loft. Darcy tightened her grip on the knife.

"Darcy!" Ryder shouted again.

"I'm here," she said, her voice weak, but she thought he heard.

"Get off her!" he roared.

"You can't have her." Ken stood, bringing her with him, and clasping her in front of him like a shield. She held the knife by her side, half-hidden in the folds of her trousers, and prayed he was too focused on Ryder to notice.

Less than six feet away, Ryder stood at the top of the stairs, both hands steadying his pistol in his hands. His eyes met Darcy's, and there was no mistaking the fear that flashed through them. He lowered the gun. "Don't do anything stupid," he said.

"You're the one who's stupid." Ken moved sideways, away from the bed. "Thinking you could have her. She belongs with me."

"I don't want to be with you!" She squirmed, but he held her so tightly her ribs ached.

"Get out of the way," Ken told Ryder. "Let us pass. And if you try anything, I'll kill her."

Why did he think *he* got to determine who she wanted to be with and what happened to her? Rage at the idea overwhelmed her. In one swift movement, she brought the knife up and plunged it into his thigh. It sank to the hilt, blood gushing. Ken screamed and released her.

Ryder grabbed her hand and thrust her away from the other man. She slid to the floor as Ryder shoved Ken against the wall, the gun held to his head. "Don't move," Ryder growled. "Don't even breathe hard."

"I'm bleeding!" Ken cried. "Do something."

"Sit down," Ryder ordered, and Ken slid to the floor.

Ryder pulled cuffs from his belt and cuffed Ken's hands behind him, then grabbed a pillow from the bed and held it over the bleeding. He looked over at Darcy. "Are you okay?"

She nodded. She felt sick and shaky, but she was alive. She had fought back. She would be okay—eventually.

He slipped a multi-tool from his belt and slid

it across the floor to her. "Can you cut the ties on your ankles?"

Though her hands were still unsteady, she managed to sever the ties and stand. "I should call 911," she said.

"Do that." He saw her hesitation and softened his voice. "I'll be okay," he said.

She went downstairs and found her phone and made the call, then collapsed on the sofa and began to sob. She didn't know why she was crying, exactly, except that it had all been so horrible, and she was so relieved it was over.

She didn't know how long it was before Ryder came to her. He wrapped her in a blanket, then drew her into his arms and held her tightly. She clung to him, sobbing. "I was s-so scared," she said through her tears.

"You were great," he said, gently kissing the side of her face. "It's over now. You're safe."

Some time after that the ambulance came, along with Travis and Gage Walker. A paramedic checked out Darcy and gave her a sedative, while two others carried a howling and complaining Ken down the narrow stairs and out to the ambulance. "What will happen to him?" Darcy asked, the medication having soothed the hard, metallic edge of fear.

"He's under arrest," Travis said. "For kidnapping and menacing and probably a half a dozen other charges we haven't sorted out yet. He'll be placed under a guard at the clinic here and when the road opens again we'll transport him to jail to await his trial."

"The road's closed again?" Ryder asked.

Travis nodded. "I'm afraid so."

"I found a snowmobile at Ken's duplex, with the windscreen shot out," Ryder said.

"He admitted he tried to run us down at Silver Pick," Darcy said. "And he was the one who pretended to be an old woman with a mastiff, who ran me off Silverthorne Road that night." She studied the faces of all three lawmen, trying to figure out what they were thinking. "I don't think he killed Kelly or the others," she said. "Maybe I'm wrong, but…"

"I don't think he killed them, either," Ryder said. "He was teaching a class full of students when Kelly was killed."

"He was supposedly at a basketball game when that truck ran Darcy off the road," Gage said.

"That one was easy enough to fake," Ryder said. "He went to the basketball game, made sure he saw and talked to a lot of people, then slipped out. People would remember he was there, but they wouldn't necessarily remember the exact time they saw him. The classroom is tougher to fake. Everyone we talked to said he was there the whole time."

"So the killer is still out there?" Darcy asked.

"Maybe," Travis said. "Or maybe he took advantage of the break in the weather and left town."

"I'm still hoping Pi and his friends saw something that will help us," Ryder said.

"So far they're still not talking," Travis said. "But

I've contacted all their parents and they all agreed this business of daring each other to do risky things has to stop. They've agreed that the boys should spend their spare time for the next few weeks doing community service."

"What kind of service?" Darcy asked.

"They can start by shoveling snow. We have a lot of it to move at the school and at the homes of elderly residents. That should keep them out of trouble."

"So what do you do about the killer?" Darcy asked.

Ryder's arm around her tightened. "We wait."

DARCY WAS SURPRISED to learn it was only a little after seven o'clock when Ryder had arrived at her house. By nine, the two of them had moved her belongings—including all four cats—into the house he rented on the other side of town. She had located the cats hidden in various places around the house—behind books on a shelf, under a sofa cushion, in a cubby in the kitchen. She dosed them all with an herbal sedative and Ryder helped her stow them in their carriers and gather their food, treats, toys and litter boxes. He didn't ask why she had changed her mind about leaving the cats at the house, merely helped her move them. She hoped it was because he understood she needed them with her. They were part of her home—and the tiny house would never feel like home again.

When they had unloaded the cats and her belongings at Ryder's place, he made macaroni and cheese and served it to her with hot tea spiked with rum. "This tastes better than anything I've ever eaten," she said, trying hard not to inhale the bowl full of orange noodles that had to be the ultimate comfort food.

"I'm not a gourmet cook, but you won't starve while you're here," he said.

She wouldn't have to be afraid while she was here, either, she thought.

After supper he persuaded her to leave the dishes until the next day, and he built a fire in the fireplace. Then they settled on the sofa and he wrapped a knitted throw around them both. "Do you want to talk about what happened?" he asked, his voice quiet.

"The sheriff said I'll need to give a statement to him tomorrow."

"You can wait until then if you like," he said. "We can try to find a victim's advocate for you to talk to, too. You don't have to tell me anything."

"I want to tell you." It was true. She laced her fingers through his. "Talking can help. I learned that before—after Jay kidnapped and raped me." It had taken her a long time—years, really—before she had been able to name the crimes done against her so boldly. But naming them was a form of taking control, she had learned.

Ryder settled her more firmly against him. "All right," he said. "I'm listening."

So she told him everything—from the moment in the kitchen through everything that had happened until his arrival at her house. Reciting the facts, along with admitting her terror in the moment, made her feel stronger. "As bad as it was, it could have been so much worse," she said. "That's one reason I don't think Ken is the one who killed Kelly and the others. He's a terrible man, but I don't think he's a murderer."

"No, I don't think so," Ryder agreed. "But I'm glad he's behind bars now—or will be, as soon as his doctors okay his release. And I'm not sure I can put into words how relieved I am that you're safe."

She turned into his arms and kissed him, a kiss that banished the chill from the last cold places within her. "Ken was right about one thing," she said.

"What is that?"

"I was wrong to insist on continuing to stay out at that isolated house by myself. Not that I would have ever accepted his offer to stay with him, but I could have gone to Stacy's."

"I'm glad you're here right now," he said.

"I'm going to stay as long as you'll have me," she said.

"How about forever?"

She stared at him, her heart having climbed somewhere into her throat. "I love you," he said. "And I want to keep on loving you. But I don't want to pressure you or control you or ever have you think I'm like Ken or Jay or anyone else who would try to hurt you."

She put her fingers over his lips. "Shhh. I know the difference between you and those others." She moved her hand and kissed the place where her fingers had been. "I love you, too," she said. "And I want to be with you." She kissed him again.

"To forever," he said and kissed her, softly and surely.

"Forever," she echoed. Saying the word was like uttering a magical incantation that opened the last lock on her heart. She felt lighter and freer—and more safe and secure—than she ever had.

* * * * *

Look for the next book in award-winning author Cindi Myers's Eagle Mountain Murder Mystery: Winter Storm Wedding miniseries, Snowbound Suspicion, *available next month.*

And don't miss the titles in the original Eagle Mountain Murder Mystery series:

Saved by the Sheriff
Avalanche of Trouble
Deputy Defender
Danger on Dakota Ridge

Available now from Harlequin Intrigue!

I N T R I G U E

Special Agent Ethan Barrow is certain his father didn't commit the crime that landed him in jail, but the only person who can help him is the daughter of the woman his father supposedly killed.

Keep reading for a sneak peek at
Criminal Behavior, *the first book in the new*
Twilight's Children *series by Amanda Stevens.*

Chapter One

Located at the end of a dead-end street, the derelict Victorian seemed to wither in the heat, the turrets and dormers sagging from time, neglect and decades of inclement weather. The gardens were lost, the maze of brick pathways broken and forgotten. The whole place wore an air of despair and long-buried secrets.

Those secrets and the steamy humidity stole Detective Adaline Kinsella's breath as she ducked under the crime-scene tape and pushed open the front door. It swung inward with an inevitable squeak, drawing a shiver.

She had the strangest sensation of déjà vu as she entered the house, and the experience both puzzled and unsettled her. She'd never been here before. Couldn't remember ever having driven down this street. But a nerve had been touched. Old memories had been triggered. If she listened closely enough, she could hear the echo of long-dead screams, but she knew that sound came straight from her nightmares.

She was just tired, Addie told herself. Five days of hiking, swimming and kayaking in ninety-degree weather had taken a toll, and now she needed a vacation from her vacation.

For nearly a week, she'd remained sequestered in her aunt's lake house without access to cable or the internet. One day had spun into another, and for the better part of the week, Addie had thought she'd found heaven on earth in the Blue Ridge Mountains. But by Thursday she'd become restless to the point of pacing on the front porch. On Friday she'd awakened early, packed up her car and headed back to Charleston, arriving just after lunch to explosive headlines and the police department abuzz with a gruesome discovery.

The details of that find swirled in her head as she hovered in the foyer. The previous owner of the house, a recluse named Delmar Gainey, had died five years earlier in a nursing home, and the property had remained vacant until an enterprising house flipper had bought it at auction. The demo crew had noticed a fusty odor, but no one had sounded an alarm. It was the smell of old death, after all. The lingering aroma of disintegrating vermin and rotting vegetation. The house had flooded at least once, allowing in the deadly invasion of mold and mildew. The structure was a public health hazard that needed to be razed, but the flipper had been adamant about renovation—until his workers had uncovered human remains behind the living room walls.

Skeletal remains had also been found behind the dining room walls and beneath the rotting floorboards in the hallway. Seven bodies hidden away inside the abandoned house and seven more buried in the backyard. Fourteen victims so far, and the search had now been extended onto the adjacent property.

"Hello?" Addie called as she moved across the foyer to the rickety staircase. The house was oppressive and sweltering. No power meant no lights and no AC. Sweat trickled down her backbone and moistened her armpits. Furtive claws scratched overhead, and the sound deepened Addie's dread. Ever since she'd heard about the Gainey house, images had bombarded her. Now she pictured the ceiling collapsing and rat bodies dropping down on her. She had a thing about rats. Spiders and snakes she could handle, but rats…

Grimacing in disgust, she moved toward the archway on her right, peeking into the shadowy space she thought might once have been the dining room. The long windows were boarded up, allowing only thin slivers of light to creep in. She could smell dust from the demolished plaster and a whiff of putrefaction. Or was that, too, her imagination? Delmar Gainey's victims had been entombed in the walls for over two decades. Surely the scent would have disintegrated by now.

A memory flitted and was gone. The nightmares still tugged…

Addie suppressed another shiver and wondered why she had come.

Don't miss
Criminal Behavior *by Amanda Stevens,*
available May 2019 wherever
Harlequin® Intrigue *books and ebooks are sold.*

www.Harlequin.com

HIEXP0419

Get 4 FREE REWARDS!

We'll send you 2 FREE Books plus 2 FREE Mystery Gifts.

Harlequin Intrigue® books feature heroes and heroines that confront and survive danger while finding themselves irresistibly drawn to one another.

FREE
Value Over
$20

"You know, that look you're giving me feels like a truth serum,"
she said. "You really don't want me to start spilling all, do you?"

Judd stayed quiet, maybe considering her question. Considering,
too, that her spilling might involve talking about this heat that was
still between them. Heat that sizzled when her eyes cleared enough
to actually see him.

He looked away from her.

Obviously, he wasn't in a spilling or hearing a spilling kind of
mood. Too bad, because a quick discussion of sizzle, followed by
some flirting, might have washed away her dark film of thoughts.

"How are you?" Cleo asked, but what she really wanted to
know was why he'd felt the need to call his sponsor.

His mouth tightened enough to let her know he didn't want to
discuss it, but it did get his gaze back on her. A long, lingering,
smoldering gaze. Though Cleo had to admit that the smoldering
part might be her own overly active imagination.

Or not.

Judd said a single word of really bad profanity, grabbed her
shoulders and dragged her to him. His mouth was on hers before

Cleo could even make a sound. It turned out, though, that no sound was necessary because she got a full, head-on slam of the heat. And this time it wasn't just simmering around them. It rolled through her from head to toe.

Now she made a sound, one of pleasure, and the years vanished. It was as if they'd picked up where they'd left off seventeen years ago, when he'd been scorching her like this in his bed.

His taste. Yes. That was the same. Maybe with a manlier edge to it, but it was unmistakably Judd. Unmistakably incredible.

Cleo felt herself moving right into the kiss. Right into Judd, too. Unfortunately, the gearshift was in the way, but she still managed some more body-to-body contact when she slid against him and into his arms.

Judd deepened the kiss, and she let him. In fact, Cleo was reasonably sure that she would have let him do pretty much anything. Yep, he'd heated her up just that much.

Apparently, though, he hadn't made himself as mindless and needy as he had her, because he pulled back, cursed again and resumed his cop's stare. Though she did think his eyes were a little blurry.

They sat there, gazes connected, breaths gusting. Waiting. Since Cleo figured her gusty breaths weren't enough to allow her to speak, she just waited for Judd to say something memorable.

"Damn," he growled.

Okay, so maybe not memorable in the way she'd wanted. Definitely not romantic. But it was such a *Judd* reaction that it made her smile. Then laugh.

She leaned in, nipped his bottom lip with her teeth. "Don't worry, Judd. I'll be gentle with you."

Don't miss
Hot Texas Sunrise *by Delores Fossen,*
available April 2019 wherever
HQN Books and ebooks are sold.

www.HQNBooks.com

PHEXPDF0419